THE FADE

THE FADE

JAMES COOPER

CEMETERY DANCE PUBLICATIONS

PUBLISHER'S NOTE
This is a work of fiction. Names, characters, places, and incidents either are the
product of the author's imagination or are used fictitiously, and any resemblance to
actual persons, living or dead, events, or locales is entirely coincidental.

THE OTHER SON

Before he fell ill, Saul's brother Philip believed he was a corpse. He complained of having lost everything and was convinced that various body parts had been taken from him in the middle of the night. He imagined himself limbless and was so immersed in his own delusion that he claimed to be able to smell his own rotting flesh and feel worms crawling through his skin. Saul was so disgusted by this ill-concealed madness that he refused to go near him for months and was secretly terrified, finding a variety of ways to keep himself permanently hidden from view.

Later, the doctors said Philip suffered from Cotard's syndrome, but by then he was deteriorating fast. It wasn't a sick joke anymore, like a screwy kid pantomiming death; it was the real thing. And before Saul had time to be truly alarmed, the memory of his brother—his *real* brother, the one he had somehow lost to an irrational disease—began to fade.

When Saul found himself starting to miss Philip's presence around the house he was mildly surprised. During the last few years they had become more and more alienated from each other and Saul had grown accustomed to safeguarding his personal space. Most of his nightmares were filled with bloated images of Philip, shuffling down the landing to his door, his brother's eyes hopelessly swelling with blood. He would whisper his psychosis in Saul's ear and tell him about his hardened arteries, his deficient heart, the tumor on his brain, and Saul would scream himself awake with the monster's name on his lips, desperate for his real brother to emerge.

The memory filled him with shame, but at the time that's all Philip ever was: a monster. The creature who lived in his house. The thing he was determined to avoid, who had stolen his brother away.

***

Their sister Amy was far more accepting. She treated Philip more humanely than anyone, and yet she had more reason than most to be afraid.

Mother had encouraged her to tend a small garden at the back of the house, on a narrow, discreetly shadowed patch of land. Saul remembered watching the two of them from the kitchen window, reveling in their time alone.

"Will anything grow there?" Amy asked. "It looks kinda dark."

"Don't worry about the darkness," Mother said. "Some plants grow beautifully in the shade. Begonias, jasmine, heliotrope." She smiled, a gesture that was becoming less common with each passing year.

At that moment, Philip trundled past, his eyes glazed over with some hidden trauma, mobilized only by his latest pathology.

"Hey, Philip! I'm gonna plant some jasmine and begoners." Amy said, the simplicity of her pleasure illuminating her pale face.

Mother chose not to correct her; saw little point in it, Saul guessed. What did it matter if a seven-year-old child mispronounced the odd word or two? Wasn't that part of their charm?

Surprisingly, Philip drew to a halt and knelt down in the soft soil, spreading his hands in the dirt. His cheeks were raw with some self-inflicted irritation and his eyes appeared sunken and lost. A stranger might have suspected he was drunk, but Father had pretty much nailed that condition for himself, and, besides, Saul knew better. It wasn't drink that addled Philip's brain; it was the faulty wiring in his head. The misfiring synapses that sparked a lunacy no one in the family could control. He couldn't help it. It was just the way he was, and they dealt with it by trying to forgive him whenever they could.

"This is where I want to be buried," he said, sieving the dirt through his hands. "In a place where the soil is soft."

Amy jumped up, shocked. "You can't!" she cried. "This is my garden. Tell him, mum! He can't be buried here, can he?"

Philip stood up and walked unsteadily back to the house, while Mother consoled a weeping Amy in her arms.

Saul tried to picture the garden in full bloom, having been nourished by Philip's withering corpse. Flowers his sister had set her heart on but could barely even name: jasmine, heliotrope, begoners.

Each morning Philip peeled away dead skin that he had feverishly worked loose in the night. It was a terrible ordeal to have to witness and Mother tried to encourage him to do it in private. If he had to do it at all, she insisted, then it must be done in the bathroom, like all the other bodily unpleasantness they endured.

It didn't much matter; they may have avoided having to watch the actual shedding, but the skin that Philip spent hours worrying from his hands and arms and feet was always left in a repulsive mound on the floor, like dirty underwear that none of them were very keen to retrieve.

Father, bearing the customary hangover, was never best pleased by these events.

"I swear, Cynth, if that boy fouls the bathroom with that shit one more time, he's out on his arse. Do you understand?"

When Father was in this kind of mood, which was, of course, most days, they had learned, by instinct it seemed, not to say a word. They quietly went about their business, buttering toast, preparing for school, and waiting for Father to explode.

"How many times has he been told? A dozen? Two dozen? I don't care how retarded the boy is, Cynth, he's got to learn. He can't treat this place like a bloody zoo. Are you listening to me, woman?"

"Of course, dear. A zoo."

Father howled helplessly. "I said not a zoo! *Not* a zoo!"

Had this ludicrous conversation taken place ten hours later, with Father in his cups, this is the point at which Mother would have received a bloody mouth. But Hangover-Father was never quite as savage as Drunk-Father, and the heat of the argument would eventually fizzle out. He would hold his head in his hands, listening to the waves pounding in his skull, and would disappear for the day to whatever watering hole he had yet to be banned from, though they were increasingly few and far between.

"You shouldn't let him speak to you like that," Saul said when Father was out of earshot, but Mother was busy making their packed lunch. Three sandwiches, an apple and a carton of Sunny Delight.

Saul liked to watch Amy tend her garden from his bedroom window and was as thrilled as she was when the first of the flowers began to bloom. Philip watched too from the garden bench as Amy tenderly turned the soil, no doubt imagining what it might feel like to have all that muck running through his hair.

When she cut her first flower, she gave the bloom to Philip and patiently helped him attach it to his coat. It was a beautiful wild violet that Mother had given to her as a gift, and which Philip, rather surprisingly, adored. He wore it with pride around the house even after it had wilted into a hideous parody of itself. When Saul asked him to remove it, Philip refused and he had repeated nightmares of his brother stalking him through the house, brandishing the battered corpse of the violet like an infected limb. Eventually, Father came to the rescue when he caught Philip staunching the blood of a self-inflicted wound with the dead petals. He was trying to offer them a little life, he said. Father told him that if he did it again, Philip wouldn't have much life left to give, and he promptly threw the flower in the bin.

The image of Philip and the wild violet, though, remained and Saul sometimes woke up with the sweet smell of it feathering his nose.

"Saul?" Amy said, while they were washing up one evening. "Why is Philip like he is? Have we done something to make him upset?"

"No, sweetheart," Saul said. "Philip's just a little different, remember? Just like mum explained."

She pondered this for a moment. "If he wants to be dead so much, why doesn't he just die?"

He had no answer to this and carried on rinsing the pots.

"*I* don't want to die," Amy said. "But I don't want to get like Philip neither. Do you think I will?"

"Of course not," Saul said. "Philip's very special. He's just sick in the head, that's all."

"But what if one of *us* gets sick in the head too? What if our skin starts peeling in the night?"

He shuddered as Amy articulated another of his recurring nightmares and playfully rubbed her on the head.

"Trust me, it'll never happen," he said, folding the tea towel and ushering her along.

But there was a part of him that wasn't so sure.

Their parents were fighting again. It usually took the form of Mother knitting in the armchair while Father screamed blue murder at her from across the room, so it was kind of one-sided, but the bile Saul felt in his stomach when it occurred had begun to fill him with dread.

It was also when Philip was at his worst. He would lie on his bed in complete silence, defined only by his homemade shroud, which had been stitched together from pilfered fabrics, and now covered him from head to toe. You could see the dull shape of his body lying motionless beneath the faded material, a small pocket of air where the mouth was occasionally disturbing the cloth.

Saul touched him once, even tried to yank him awake, but to all intents and purposes he was dead. When the shroud fell away Philip's eyes were wide open. What he saw was anybody's guess.

One morning, Philip announced over breakfast that his body was turning to stone. He said he could no longer raise his arms above his head and he would soon be unable to walk.

Mother continued pouring milk on her cereal and Amy and Saul immersed themselves in the TV.

"What's this?" Father said, appearing clean-shaven and refreshed at the door.

"Nothing," Mother said quickly. "Philip was just telling us he feels a little unwell today, that's all."

Father grunted. "What's new?" he said, taking a seat.

"I'm turning to stone," Philip said calmly. "I can feel it. My digestive system, my insides. Everything."

Mother sighed, anticipating Father's response and Saul rolled his eyes, feeling a rush of nausea and hate.

"Philip, you are so full of shit!" he said. "Why can't you just keep your fucking mouth shut for a change!"

"Saul!" Mother said, turning on him with an anger he didn't expect. "Don't you ever use language like that in this house."

"Father does!" Saul blurted, "All the fucking time. We hear him when you think we're asleep."

Mother looked shocked and turned to Father for support. When his hand caught Saul on the side of the head he felt a momentary pain and then a swell of relief that Philip's lunacy had been temporarily forgot.

"Go to your room!" Father shouted. "All of you!"

Mother nodded her head and they disappeared up the stairs, Philip dragging his petrified feet.

⸻

The best time to catch Father in a good mood was Saturday afternoon. He lay on the sofa drinking Stella and betting on the horses by phone, but for a few hours, before the beer and the losses took their toll, he could almost be fun to be around. He was a proper Father then, just for a brief spell, and if he was drowning his sorrows and racking up debt at the same time, what did it matter? It would only affect the kids later on, when the horror of what he'd become kicked in.

It was a Saturday afternoon when Saul noticed him with Amy, kneeling before her wonderful garden with his arm around her shoulders, seemingly in the middle of a prayer. He was pointing to some of the flowers and Amy was delighting in telling him everything she'd learned about each one. They looked happy, purely happy, and Saul wondered how long their display of affection might last. The garden had facilitated moments of tenderness that they simply weren't accustomed to, and he was waiting for the bubble to burst.

It was inevitable, of course, that eventually Philip would try to kill himself. His consultant, Dr. Bradshaw, had warned them as much. Mother had been very conscientious in stripping the house of any materials that might be deemed dangerous, including knitting needles, lead pencils, kitchen knives and so on. But how could you really provide a safe domestic environment for someone like Philip? Short of locking him in a padded cell, it was impossible. Naturally, Mother blamed herself, and being the kind of family that they were, they let it happen. They did nothing to try and ease the guilt that was progressively eating her away.

Amy found him, of course; another tragedy for which Mother was never able to fully forgive herself, though if she were here now she'd probably disagree. Saul believed she tried, but he could see the pain in her eyes. It was as though some private trauma was unfolding in the distance, and she was unable to make up the ground. She stayed like that for a long time, as long as Saul could remember, irreversibly damaged by her own flesh and blood, the weight of the family's dysfunction too much for any one person to bear.

It was Amy, though, who suffered the most. No seven-year-old girl should have to walk into the bathroom and see the blood of her brother spilled across the floor. By this stage, Philip had abused his body to such a degree that it was barely recognizable as human. There were scars, abrasions, and sundry other deformities that had degraded him beyond repair. It was, Dr. Bradshaw informed Mother, all part of a process of 'derealization' that Philip seemed to be experiencing, and, in retrospect, it was little wonder he had tried to reduce himself to an actual corpse. He had been telling them he was dead for so long now they had simply become inured to it. The only way to convince them was with this desperately insane display.

The incident was still fresh in Saul's mind, and would remain lodged there for quite some time. He heard Amy scream and ran upstairs, expecting to see her in some kind of physical distress. Mother had got there first and was busy securing the bathroom door, while Amy, ashen-faced, continued to scream down the house.

"What is it?" Saul yelled, wrapping his arms around his sister and burying her head in his chest.

"It's Philip," Mother said, looking visibly shaken. "I think he's dead."

The statement, after hearing it from Philip himself for so long, sounded powerless and mildly amusing, as though Mother was doing her best to cheer everyone up.

She nodded her head. "I need you to take Amy downstairs," she said, "and call Dr. Bradshaw. Okay? Then sit with your sister and do your best to calm her down. Give her tea with lots of honey. It'll soothe her and help her to sleep. Blankets are in the cupboard under the stairs."

Then she turned her back on them, slid open the bathroom door, and squeezed herself in. Saul had a sickening glimpse of something red scribbled across the floor before his Mother's body impeded the view. When she finally shut the door, it closed with a terrible *snick*, trapping his mother inside.

When she came out, much later, with Dr. Bradshaw and the paramedics, Saul could tell she had been changed. She took his hand and smiled reassuringly, but there was blood on her face and in her hair. She looked monstrous and he tried to pull away, but she clung on, breathing heavily, in need of someone innocent to love.

They moved house; they had to. None of them dared venture into the bathroom, except Father, of course, who was usually too full of piss and liquor to care. Mother never set foot in the room again. She bathed as best she could in the kitchen sink, used the old outhouse when she needed the loo and twice a week drew a bath in old Mrs. Pritchard's house two doors down. When they moved, it was Mother who was most relieved.

Philip spent two weeks in hospital after he tried to kill himself and another six being treated by Dr. Bradshaw at The Collingwood Foundation. When he emerged, he was slower, weaker and paler, like fodder circling the pen, waiting to be zapped in the brain. Father told Saul that Philip had received a special treatment called electroconvulsive therapy to try and make him normal again and it had worked better than any of them had hoped.

But he didn't look normal; he looked sick. There was no

denying the crazy part had been removed, but that was all Philip had left and now he shuffled around like a caricature of the walking dead.

Saul visited the library and looked up electroconvulsive therapy on the computer. The screen flashed like a light bulb had gone on above its head and then showed him this:

Electroshock (ECT) involves the production of a grand mal convulsion, similar to an epileptic seizure, by passing from 70 to 600 volts of electric current through the brain for 0.5 to 4 seconds. Before application, ECT subjects are typically given anesthetic, tranquillizing and muscle-paralyzing drugs to reduce fear, pain, and the risk (from violent muscle spasms) of fractured bones (particularly of the spine, a common occurrence in the earlier history of ECT before the introduction of muscle paralyses). The ECT convulsion usually lasts from thirty to sixty seconds and may produce life-threatening complications, such as apnea and cardiac arrest. The convulsion is followed by a period of unconsciousness of several minutes' duration. Electroshock is usually administered in hospitals because they are equipped to handle emergency situations which often develop during or after an ECT session. Brain damage, memory loss and mental disability are routine distinguishing results.

He looked at the screen and felt physically sick. How could his own parents approve of such a thing? He ran home, barreled up the stairs and stood panting at the threshold of Philip's room. His brother was lying inert on the bed, a sliver of drool forming at the corner of his mouth. Saul wanted to hug him but was too afraid. Instead, he tried to imagine what Philip had endured; wasn't at all surprised that he longed to be dead.

As they settled into their new home, unpacking the same worries, the same fears, the same endless hostilities, Philip formed his first and only relationship beyond the family.

One of the neighbors, an old man named Bernard Putts, was an extremely skilled craftsman, a carpenter by trade, who could carve an angel from the bough of a tree. He worked from home and could be heard toiling in his converted outhouse late into the night, persuading his lathe to sing. He rarely spoke and was reluctant to look anyone in the eye, but his skills were in great demand, often forcing him to turn work away that he knew he wouldn't have time to complete. He worked tirelessly and would have done so in any circumstance, but his gift was a good provider and he lived a frugal but comfortable life. He was an artist, Mother explained, and his medium was wood. She and Amy were in awe of him from the moment they arrived.

Not Philip, though, who deferred to no one and freely bore the marks of a differentiated life. Perhaps it was this that appealed to Bernard Putts, the fact that Philip was a kindred spirit, a soul consumed by some ponderous obsession that had driven him to pursue an existence that no one in his family could possibly understand.

Ultimately, it didn't really matter; Philip had wandered over into Bernard's yard one day and a pattern had been irrevocably defined. He would stand watching Bernard at work, sometimes for hours at a time, and the aching sadness that he seemed to exude would slowly and miraculously retreat. Mother had tried to discourage him, had even apologized to Bernard on Philip's behalf, but the old man had just smiled and said, "He's happy here", before patiently returning to work.

Saul couldn't quite understand Philip's fascination back then, nor Bernard's passive acceptance of the intrusion, but he had developed a clearer perspective of it, and it filled him with a warmth he could barely describe.

They were happy; purely happy. It was as simple, and as complicated, as that.

If they ever spoke to each other Saul certainly didn't hear of it, though Bernard would provide Philip with sandwiches and squash when he stopped for lunch, and a chair when the weather grew warm. In turn, Philip would take Bernard peculiarly-shaped pieces of wood he managed to dislodge from unseen places around the house, which Bernard would patiently stockpile until he had enough to make Philip a bird in mid-flight or a leaping tiger or some other impossible treasure that Philip would lovingly arrange in his room.

It was a strange relationship, certainly, but it was beautiful too, in its way, undemanding and secure, until the day Mother went round to Bernard's house and found Philip lying in a hand-made coffin, his dreams of extinction complete.

Mother was mortified, but for all her anxiety it seemed that Philip was perfectly at peace. The coffin was exquisitely crafted and had been lined with crushed velvet to better accommodate the body inside. Apparently, when Mother made the discovery, Philip had his eyes closed and his hands drawn creepily across his chest, playing dead to the sound of Bernard's beguiling lathe.

It should have ended there, the bizarre friendship having reached a point at which it was impossible not to become concerned. But when he was forbidden to enter Bernard's yard, Philip invoked the mother of all rages and began destroying every wooden item in his room, whereupon Father used said items to beat him to within an inch of his life.

It was an ugly display and it completely changed the balance of power in the house. Father realized how close he had come to doing serious bodily harm to his own son and became much more subdued, a whisky-addled figure in the corner of the room whose life had been frittered away. Mother remained as impassive as ever, lost somewhere in the hinterland between her troubled marriage and what she'd imagined it to be, and Amy and Saul began to spend more time at school, finding countless ways to avoid going home.

As for Philip, his privileges were eventually restored and he returned to Bernard's workshop as though he'd never been away. He assumed his place in the hand-made coffin and fell asleep to the dull *clink* of the old radiator rattling the pipes.

But when he woke up, he had coughed up blood, and his eyes were yellow and sick. He felt weak, he said, his teeth were cold, and he could no longer stand the sight of his own skin. When they took him to the hospital, he kept his eyes closed for the entire journey, holding Mother's hand and making a noise through his teeth like a lathe.

Father drove Amy and Saul to the hospital without uttering a word and Saul became increasingly worried that they'd be pulled over by the police for speeding. He reeked of booze and he was veering erratically across the road, though it was difficult to know whether this was a by-product of the whisky or whether it was just panic, which, up to that point, had been potent enough to silence them all.

"I can't stop thinking about Philip," Amy said finally. "Can I listen to a story? It might take my mind off everything."

"No stories," Father said, peering at the road with ridiculous intensity. "We're nearly there."

Saul reached into the back seat and briefly touched Amy's hand, communicating his own nervousness rather than the hope she was looking for, which was hardly reassuring. He offered a weak smile instead and turned to face the grubby windscreen, which was throwing mottled bursts of the landscape in their direction, inviting them to rearrange the pieces.

"Would it hurt?" Saul asked, prepared to risk Father's wrath on Amy's behalf. "It's just a story."

"What the hell do we need stories for?" he said. "Isn't this shit dramatic enough for you? Now shut up, both of you. I need to concentrate."

Saul fell silent, realizing that this wasn't the time to pick a fight. Father was unpredictable enough when he was steamed; what he might be like when he was drunk *and* fraught was anybody's guess. Now certainly wasn't the time to find out, with the steering wheel already shaking dangerously between his trembling hands. A braver man might have pushed it a little further, but kids are rarely brave, not in reality. There's always too much to lose. They may be fearless (sometimes foolishly so) but not brave. Not in a world where kids are driven to hospitals by drunk fathers to visit brothers who dream of being dead. It's just too much to ask.

So Saul sat there, feeling angry and hurt, staring at the blurred countryside, wondering how foolish he dared become.

He looked at Father, his eyes red and beady, his jowls heavy with sweat, and realized that at some point in the journey this man he'd only ever known from a distance had changed. It was all he could do to point the car in the right direction and drive. Father, who Saul had always taken for granted, had a look in his eye that he knew well, and he felt assailed by a crippling sadness, the kind that settled with a deep ache in the empty chambers of the heart.

It was unmistakable. Father was afraid, and Saul suddenly realized just how angry and alone he'd become.

When they arrived at the hospital Mother had already assumed the customary position of the traumatized relative, seated in an orange plastic seat in a non-descript corridor with a look of horror inhabiting her face. A flurry of nurses and doctors tried to spread an air of calm assurance, but it had little impact on those whose lives were about to be changed, and in truth, they would have been uncommonly surprised if it ever did.

Saul noticed how Mother tried to catch Father's eye as he sat down, but neither of them really knew where to begin, and the gesture passed unnoticed, except by Saul, and he wondered why it was that he had the misfortune of observing these things, why he had to live with the casual rejections his parents seemed unable to sense. Even now, in a time of family crisis, they were struggling to connect. Years of marriage, instead of empowering them and investing them with a shared perspective, had done little more than betray their fundamental uncertainty of one another. Saul wanted to cry. Not just because his brother was losing the good fight, but because his parents seemed to be, too. They had been drifting apart for so long he had barely even noticed it before; it was like watching a clock run backwards, the hands imperceptibly turning further and further away from where they should be. He stared at his father and wondered what he was thinking about, tried to imagine what might be going on inside his head. He seemed to have sobered up fast, but Saul knew that this was probably because the booze had been shocked out of his system. Hospitals had a way of doing that to people. You got a jolt of reality just stepping into the place. Death hung in the air; you could smell it as soon as you walked in.

Saul looked down at Amy, who was slumped in one of the plastic chairs beside Mother, and rested a hand against her cheek.

"Don't worry," he said. "He won't be in here long. Philip's a fighter."

Amy glanced up and Saul noticed how wide her eyes were, how bright her pupils seemed in the harsh artificial light.

"What if he don't want to come back?" she said. "What if he likes it here?"

"No one likes it here," Saul said softly, revealing his own aversion to the place.

"Philip might," she whispered, and he realized he had nothing to say, because she was right. Philip could easily lose himself in such a place. He would find death at every turn and be comfortable with it. It would be the perfect venue to await the inevitable fading of the light.

They sat there in silence, each mulling over their own private horror, as the hospital staff fluttered back and forth along the corridor. Eventually a doctor approached them. He was tall and Saul noticed that he had large, clean hands. He also thought he looked tired. He tried to imagine working long shifts in such emotionally fraught conditions. He wondered how many people had died in the hospital since they'd arrived and it occurred to him that there must be a room where they deposited the bodies. He tried to picture what it might be like inside and vaguely considered whether they stacked people in steel drawers like in the shows he and Mother sometimes watched on TV.

"Mr. and Mrs. Langley?" the doctor said. He was leaning forward and smiling. He held out his large hand and Saul watched as Father accepted it like a drowning man reaching for support.

"I'm Dr. Crozier," he said. He shook Mother's hand and then indicated an open door a few feet along the corridor. "Shall we?"

Father led the way into a cluttered office and the others followed, with Dr. Crozier bringing up the rear. He closed the door and seated himself behind a cheap, laminated desk. He plucked a red lollipop from a bowl and smiled as he offered it to Amy, who took it and held it in her hand.

"How is he?" Mother said. She was perched on the edge of her seat, brow furrowed, expecting the worst. Saul stood behind her and placed a hand on her shoulder. She reached back without looking and took hold of it. Father glanced across and Saul felt a rush of pity for him. He wanted to place a hand on Father's shoulder too, just to remind him that his other son was nearby, but he was too afraid. Even at a time like this there was something in the man's eyes that held him back.

"We think he'll be fine," Dr. Crozier said, and Mother released a deep breath that she was barely aware of having held.

"Thank God," she muttered. She turned to Father and he nodded once and briefly closed his eyes.

"What caused it?" Mother asked.

Dr. Crozier patted a large file on his desk and sighed.

"We think it was a by-product of the electro-shock," he said, "though it's difficult to be sure. Certainly we can't find anything else that might have caused it. There's no evidence of a growth and no underlying pathology, other than the one Dr. Sharman has already diagnosed."

Dr. Crozier paused for a moment and opened the file. I saw Philip's name printed on the front. He spent a minute or two flipping through the pages and then said: "Did the doctors at Collingwood explain to you the possible complications of ECT?"

Mother nodded. "They told us about memory loss," she said.

"And would you say Philip's memory has been adversely affected?"

Mother and Father exchanged a knowing glance.

"It's not always easy to tell with Philip," Father said. "He tends to live in his own world. What the hell goes on there is hard to say."

Dr. Crozier nodded and steepled his fingers on the desk.

"What kind of things does he talk about?"

"Being dead!" Amy said, leaning against Mother's arm. "That's the only thing he thinks about, isn't it Saul?"

"Hush now," Mother said to Amy. She looked a little embarrassed and turned back to the doctor. "He's got better since the treatments," she said. "He's not quite so..." She scrabbled around for the right word and Father helped Mother out by quietly muttering: "Intense."

She nodded and sat back, content to leave it at that.

"Okay," Dr. Crozier said, rising to his feet. "I think I have enough to be getting on with. Why don't we pay a visit to the man of the hour, see how he's coming along?"

Philip had been given a private room, and Saul suspected it was because the doctors thought he was too crazy to be cared for on one of the wards. As they walked down the corridor the nurses eyed them with suspicion, as though it were somehow the family's fault that Philip had developed into such a damaged soul. Father glared back, pleased to have located an enemy at which he could direct some of his anger. Saul, though, felt sorry for them; they had to minister to Philip, who could be difficult at the best of times. How much worse might he be once he realized he'd been admitted into hospital without his consent?

Mother entered the room first and emitted a single sob as she approached Philip's bed and gave him a hug. He shrugged her off and glanced up as the rest of the family trooped in. He failed to acknowledge them and turned instead to Dr. Crozier, who was quietly closing the door. Saul noticed that Philip had a clipboard in his hand and was poring over a complicated medical chart.

"Blood pressure's forty over ten," he said. "Way too low."

Mother looked to Dr. Crozier, alarmed. The doctor shook his

head and whispered, "If that were true he'd be in a coma." He offered her another of those disarming smiles and placed his large hands in the pockets of his white coat. "Philip kept interfering with the charts," he went on, "so it seemed best to give him one of his own. It seems to have calmed him down a little. Don't worry, the chart's completely blank. I assure you that whatever he's reading on there is completely fabricated. Another one of those trips to his imaginary world, perhaps."

Philip tapped the clipboard and looked hard at Dr. Crozier.

"I have Addison's disease," he said. "It's been confirmed."

Mother glanced at Dr. Crozier and he patiently shook his head.

"What makes you say that, Philip?" he said, indulging him.

"I asked Dr. Caton to perform a Synachten test. I have primary adrenal failure. It's right here in black and white." Another tap of the clipboard was followed by a look of moral certitude, as though Philip was daring Dr. Crozier to prove him wrong.

Father looked away, disgusted, and muttered something under his breath.

Dr. Crozier ignored him and produced a small container from his pocket.

"Addison's can be controlled, Philip, with steroids. We'll start you on 15mg of hydrocortisone three times a day. Okay?"

He poured him a glass of water, then handed Philip the container and encouraged him to take the single white pill inside. Philip took the tablet and washed it down with the water. He placed the clipboard on the bed, dropped back onto his pillow and closed his eyes. Saul noticed that Amy was clutching Mother's skirt, more afraid than ever of her brother's crumbling mental state.

Mother leaned towards Dr. Crozier and pointed at the plastic container.

The doctor smiled. "Nothing sinister," he said. "Just a little something to help him sleep."

Saul looked across at Father and saw him discreetly wipe a tear from his eye. He quickly averted his gaze, terrified of being caught. He looked instead at the darkening sky through the window, and saw the ghostly reflection of his brother in the glass. It looked like he was fading away.

2

MR. WHIPPY

Hilary Bunce turned on the chimes, pulled the van into the clearing, and watched the children run towards him as though greeting a long-lost friend. This is what he loved about driving the ice-cream van: it *normalized* him. For a brief time, it made him feel just like everyone else.

He parked up, maneuvered his large frame out of the seat, and pulled back the glass screen. The children were already clamoring amongst themselves, pointing at the images of iced lollies and cones stuck to the side of the van.

Bunce wiped a few rogue strands of hair across his balding pate, what his Pa liked to call the 'Charlton Whip', and smiled down at the waiting throng. His head was round, like a cue ball, and seemed to perch awkwardly on sloping shoulders, giving the impression that he had no neck. When he smiled his lips seemed to jut forward, like an old man eliciting a gurn, and his brown eyes were set too far back in the sockets, giving the impression of a nocturnal animal unused to the light. He wore a white apron bearing the image of an astronaut and the logo *In Space No One Can Eat Ice-Cream*. None of the children understood what it meant, but occasionally one or two of the parents did. Bunce would see them smile and send their children running towards him, coins clutched tightly in sweaty hands. The apron normalized him too. They turned away without giving him a second glance. They trusted him with their kids, even if only for a moment, and that suited Hilary Bunce just fine. He was the fat man with the funny apron who served their children ice-cream. Sometimes he would wave to the distant parents, eager to reassure them, and without even looking at him they would casually wave back. Then they were gone and, though some of them might remember the apron, the face of the ice-cream man would stay with them for about as long as it took to walk back to the car.

Bunce looked down at the kids and spread his podgy hands either side of the counter. It was hot and the children looked slick with sweat. He wiped his brow and felt his practiced smile slip a little. It had been a long day. Surprisingly, he yearned to be home. He leaned forward and showed a mouthful of crooked yellow teeth.

"Righto," he said to the first little boy in the queue. "Time to choose."

He pulled in to the driveway of Pa's farmhouse and parked the van in the rear barn. He spent half an hour cleaning out the pipes and clogged channels of the ice cream machine, before emptying the day's takings from the till. He didn't bother counting it as every penny of it went to Pa. He simply stuffed the notes into his pocket and the coins into a plastic tub. He then climbed out of the van, locked the barn doors, dodged the inquisitive chickens infesting the yard, and entered the house.

He took off his apron and hung it on the peg in the utility room. He could hear Pa and Fliss talking in the kitchen, and he paused for a moment to see if the conversation was about him. He smiled to himself in the gloom, his upper lip shriveling like a salted slug; the conversation was *never* about him. Since Pa had invited Fliss to move in with them, the dynamic of the family had changed. Everything was suddenly all about her.

Bunce had heard a rumor that Fliss had killed off her last husband and buried his body in the cotton mill at the north end of town. It was a thrilling notion and a large part of him wanted it to be true. He had even ventured into the mill late at night and begun mapping its interior, hoping to stumble upon something incriminating he could lovingly present to Pa. The only things he found were syringes, broken crates and smashed beer bottles where the local kids had themselves hidden away to indulge their perfectly run-of-the-mill vices. All pretty tame stuff. After a few hours of fruitless searching, Bunce came away fairly satisfied that, if Fliss *had* done away with her last husband, she hadn't deposited the body in the mill.

He turned his head towards the kitchen and listened to Pa's rumbling voice, the mere sound of which had the capacity to freeze Bunce's blood whenever Pa thought he'd done something bad.

"They'll turn up," he said. "They always do. You probably dropped them last time you took them off."

Bunce heard Fliss sigh and imagined her throwing Pa a withering glance.

"I haven't dropped them, Bill. They've been taken. There's only one person in this family stupid enough to do that, and we both know who it is, don't we?"

Bunce waited out the silence. Fliss was referring to him, and he felt a sudden heat in his cheeks. If something had gone missing it was more likely that Gilly was responsible; his psychotic younger brother, the boy who, in the eyes of Pa and his new partner, could seemingly do no wrong. Bunce bridled as he pictured

Gilly's lean, unblemished face. Showed how much Pa and Fliss knew. Gilly was like a trapped rat in a coal shed and would gnaw through anything to work himself free. That Bunce hated him made life difficult enough; that Gilly hated him right back made the situation considerably worse.

"Hilary won't have taken them," Pa said, surprising Bunce by standing up for him in the face of Fliss's insistence. "What the hell would he want with a pair of bloody earrings?"

Bunce heard Pa turn the page of a newspaper, probably in the hope that the gesture might bring the conversation to a timely halt. Bunce smiled; he knew Fliss all too well. Pa would have no such luck, he was sure.

"That boy creeps me out," she said. "He probably wears them late at night when we're both asleep and pretends to be me. Like a pervert or something."

Pa laughed. "Bloody hell, Fliss! You really think so?"

Bunce heard Fliss reach over and imagined her punching Pa in the arm. "I'm serious," she said. "He lurks around the house. You must have seen him, right?"

Pa laughed again. "*Lurks*, does he? Jesus Christ! You've been reading too much twaddle, Fliss."

Bunce chose this moment to announce himself and Pa looked up, annoyed.

"Have you got Fliss's earrings?" he said. "She's driving me nuts over here. Reckons you stole the damn things."

Bunce shook his head and walked towards the fridge. He opened the door, pulled out a 7Up, pushed in the tab, and began to drink.

"Satisfied?" Pa said.

Fliss stared at the wall, refusing to look at either of them, and then marched out of the kitchen, indignant. Pa fell silent and turned back to his paper. Bunce took another swig from the can. He was invisible again, just how he liked it. What he privately called the Fade. He felt at home here; he knew every nook and cranny of the place. This was his territory. This was where Hilary Bunce was king.

He turned to leave the kitchen and suddenly heard gunshots coming from the room above. Gilly was shooting at the chickens again. Pa didn't so much as raise an eyebrow. He had seen it all before. He licked a finger, turned over a page of the newspaper, and calmly continued to read.

Bunce ran out the door and looked up at the rear of the farmhouse. Gilly was leaning out of his bedroom window, dressed in full combat gear, taking potshots at the outraged chickens. He was targeting them with a Winchester Black Shadow; several of them already lay dead in the yard.

"What the hell are you doing?" Bunce called up.

"The little bastards were taunting me," Gilly said, the shotgun partially covering his face. "They needed to be taught a lesson."

He pumped another cartridge into the chamber, drew the stock into his shoulder, leveled the barrel at the scurrying chickens, and blew another of them clean into the air. All that came fluttering down was a pulped mess of bloody feathers and eviscerated muck.

"Isn't this a little extreme?" Bunce said. He glanced around the yard; it was littered with the splattered debris of Gilly's insane retribution. The remaining chickens were clucking in terror. There was nowhere for them to run; they had become moving targets dancing to the tune of Gilly's shotgun.

He lowered the firearm and stared at Bunce. He wore his customary expression of bewilderment and disdain, as though his brother's very existence both puzzled and annoyed him. He raised the Winchester again and turned it in Bunce's direction until the barrel was pointed at his chest.

"You treading with the enemy?" he said.

Bunce lifted his hands in exasperation. "There *is* no enemy!" he shouted up at Gilly. "There's just you shooting at Pa's damn chickens!"

"Look into their eyes, douchebag. These fuckers are messing with us. It's time Johnny Jihad had a taste of his own medicine."

Bunce shook his head and exhaled loudly. He stared up at Gilly, a young man who had watched *Jarhead* several dozen times more than was healthy for him, and realized that his brother had slipped into a bruise-colored world that was probably as terrifying, and as empty, as the Fade.

He watched Gilly lower a pair of goggles over his eyes and then draw aim on another innocent bird. This time he missed and the cartridge exploded into the cobbled yard. Shards of stone flew into the air and Bunce protected his face with a raised arm.

"Quit it!" he said. "You'll end up doing something you'll regret."

Gilly stared down at him through the goggles.

"Collect your shit and move out, soldier," he said. "There's a heap of work to be done."

Bunce went back inside the farmhouse and found the kitchen empty. He could still hear Gilly unleashing hell on the poultry stock, but with the back door closed it sounded like an old truck backfiring. He tried to tune it out. He handcombed what remained of his hair across his scalp and moved across to the refrigerator. He opened the door and let the cold air wash over him. It felt good. He needed cooling down after his encounter with Gilly. The man's foolishness made his blood boil.

He removed a slab of cheddar cheese from the fridge, crossed the room and seated himself at the kitchen table, where Pa had been reading the newspaper. It lay open at a story about the perils of urban foxes. There was a picture of one rooting through the disturbed contents of a green dustbin. The animal had sensed the photographer and glanced up just as the picture was about to be taken; its eyes were yellow with reflected light from the flash.

Bunce carefully peeled back the cling film on the cheese and tore off a large chunk with his bare hand. It smelled strong and fresh. He bit into it and sank back into the chair, laying a hand on his heaving paunch. He glanced down at it and frowned. He hated being fat, but couldn't bring himself to stop eating calorie-rich foods like the damn cheese.

Fliss entered the kitchen and stared at the half-eaten chunk of cheese in his hand. She looked disgusted. Bunce was mildly surprised to see her standing there, but he shouldn't have been; she had a way of padding around the house with the stealth of a Burmese cat.

"Have you no manners?" she said. "How hard would it be to equip yourself with a knife and a plate when...*gorging* on your father's food?"

"It's my food, too," Bunce said. He tried to stop his voice from trembling like a ten-year-old boy's. "I work as hard as anyone round here. Ask Pa."

Fliss gave a derisive laugh. "You mean driving around in that ridiculous van? Hardly what I'd call working. And if this little scene is anything to go by, I suspect you eat more than you sell. I bet you're dreaming of it right now, aren't you? All that beautifully soft ice-cream..."

Bunce felt his cheeks grow hot and he glanced down at the half-eaten lump of cheese.

"At least I contribute to the household," he said. "Unlike some."

Before he could gauge the effect of his words, Fliss crossed the kitchen, leant over the kitchen table and swiped her hand across his cheek. Bunce could feel the stinging stroke of her nails as they raked his skin, could see the blind rage in her wide, unblinking eyes.

"*How dare you!*" she said. "I've done more to make your father happy than you ever will! This family was nothing before I got here. *Nothing!* Do you hear me? Now look at it."

Bunce leant back in his chair. It wasn't at all clear what Fliss wanted him to see. The family seemed as dysfunctional as ever. Was she trying to suggest that she'd changed it for the better? If that was the case, Bunce must have been missing something. In his opinion, all that had changed was that Pa had become increasingly depressed. Bunce had caught him one night, long after everyone had gone to bed and the farmhouse had grown cold, sitting in the lounge, poring over old photographs of his first wife. Worse still, Pa had looked ashamed that he'd been caught, as though the act of reminiscing was forbidden. Bunce had quietly crept away. The next morning neither of them was able to look the other in the eye.

Bunce stared now at Fliss and watched the rage slowly drain from her face. She looked at him and smiled, the curl of her lip rising.

"You're pathetic," she said softly. "I hope you know that, Hilary. Your Pa thinks so too. He told me."

Bunce shook his head.

"That's not true," he said. He held a hand up to his cheek and was startled to discover that Fliss's wild swipe had drawn blood. "You're just saying that to try and hurt me, but it won't work because it's just not true. I know it's not."

Fliss sighed, as though expressing her sincerest regret. "Oh, but it is, sweetie. He told me when we first hooked up. Said it was like living with a retard. He told me when I first met the family not to expect too much."

Bunce continued shaking his head, trying not to listen. He closed his eyes and heard a ringing inside his skull, which was still rocking from Fliss's unexpected blow. He visualized her leaping forward and heard her say *You're pathetic* over and over again, until he felt like reaching up and tearing the image from his brain. It was eventually replaced by a shifting montage, a collection of thoughts that made Bunce feel nauseous: Gilly in his combat gear shooting at the chickens, a sneering child leaning up at him in the van, Pa disappearing in the woods at the back of the house. Fliss was right; he *was* pathetic. The world turned and Bunce could feel its creeping contempt.

He opened his eyes and stared across the table at her.

"You really shouldn't have hit me," he said. "Pa won't like it one bit."

Fliss laughed, and Bunce thought it sounded like a chair being scraped across a wooden floor.

"You think you know him," she said, "but I'll be surprised if he even listens to you. He has other things on his mind right now. You, he's barely even aware of. Haven't you noticed that?" She leant towards him again and added: "Are you too dumb to see what's right in front of your face?"

Bunce looked away, unable to maintain eye contact with the woman, and Fliss pulled away, failing to conceal her disgust. She had dug the knife in deep and twisted it far enough for one day; now she had grown bored. Bunce could see it in her eyes. The petty cruelty she had inflicted had energized her and now she wanted to move on to something more palatable; something that didn't involve staring at Bunce's miserable face.

She turned away and began walking from the room.

"Remember," she said over her shoulder. "Next time use a

plate. Otherwise I'll have Gilly throw you in the sty with the rest of the pigs."

She flounced out of the kitchen and disappeared down the hall. Bunce watched her go and then glanced down at the chunk of cheese in his hand. The sight of it suddenly made him feel sick. He walked over to the pedal bin, depressed the lever, and threw it in. He stared at the tips of his fingers, then raised them to his nose. There was a strong odor emanating from the skin. Bunce thought it smelled like failure.

Bunce sat at his bedroom window and stared down at the yard. Dusk was descending, marking the landscape with a sense of renewed mystery. He peered beyond the fields and saw the distant woodland, a black, muscular weight on the horizon.

Down below Pa was cleaning up the mess Gilly had made earlier. His head was bent forward and his back bowed, as he stooped to collect the splattered remains of the birds. He moved quietly from chicken to chicken, scooping up what was left with a hand shovel and depositing the mess in a black refuse bag. If Pa had at any point reprimanded Gilly for his insanity, Bunce hadn't heard it. Neither had he heard Pa instruct Gilly to attend to the filth in the yard. As usual, Pa had simply assumed responsibility for it, without a word of complaint, and it made Bunce feel as though the system had failed him yet again. He resented Pa's acceptance of Gilly's psychotic behavior. He wanted to see his father—no, *expected* to see his father—assert his authority. He wanted to see Gilly taken in hand. The usual approach of excusing his gratuitous conduct with the same silent validation filled Bunce with a kind of mindless rage. It hurt him to think that Gilly could pass through life without being challenged, while Bunce's every breath seemed to be drawn against the odds. It made him realize how uniquely alone he was. Had he been the one shooting the damn chickens he had no doubt that both Pa and Fliss would have confined him to his room for a week.

He glanced down and watched Pa work his way around the yard. He wondered if he was happy and watched his father's face, trying to see behind the implacable features to the man behind the mask. It was no good; Pa never gave anything away. His face remained impassive, a blank slate upon which was writ the dull measure of his life. When Bunce looked at Pa he could see the years of labor stacked up in the creases of his face. He was not an easy man to read and never had been, but he suspected that the slumped figure trawling the yard gathering chicken guts and feathers was far from happy. He looked tired and lost, Bunce thought. He caught a fleeting glimpse of Pa's eyes as he glanced at the farmhouse and it occurred to him that what he was seeing was a man in pain. It was well concealed, true, but Bunce thought he had witnessed it nonetheless.

Once Pa had finished clearing up the entrails he set the shovel and the black bag against the coal bunker and reached for the hose clamped to the wall. He unspooled it, turned on the tap and gave the cobbles a long, cold blast. Bunce watched the remaining filth sluice away in the runnels of water. When this was complete, Pa went inside for a few minutes and returned with an industrial-strength detergent, which he liberally sprayed all over the yard. The stench of the compound rose into the air and reached Bunce's nostrils, even behind the glass. He winced at the chemical smell and covered his mouth and nose. When he next leaned forward, expecting to see Pa carrying the black bag and the shovel towards the barn, he saw only an empty space. The bag and the shovel remained propped against the coal bunker.

He raised his head and looked out across the darkening land. There, trudging across the unploughed field in his heavy work boots, was Pa. He was heading for the woods. He was walking with a steady, purposeful stride. His arms swung with a perfect rhythm; his head was lowered, gauging the uneven ground beneath his feet. In his left hand Bunce thought he could see a small container. It looked like a jewelry box. He squinted his eyes. It looked familiar, like the one Ma used to have on her dressing table. Could that be right? He looked again, expecting to correct himself. There was a lot of ground between him and Pa. Wasn't it possible that he had simply made a mistake? He frowned; more than possible, he thought. Pa was getting further away with every step and the features of the box were becoming increasingly difficult to define. He tried to picture it in his mind, drawn from memory: a small brown box with an intricately carved pattern that had always reminded Bunce of the secret paths he used to explore through the trees that surrounded the farm. He remembered placing his finger on the box once and tracing one of the meandering loops, following the mesmeric spirals cut into the surface of the wood. He'd felt a light tingle in the nerve endings at the tip of his finger, as though the box was trying to communicate with him. *Hello, Mr. Bunce. How are you today? Still feeling a little blue? Let me show you something that'll cheer you up. Open my lid and you'll see the true path to happiness. You'll never feel alone or invisible again...*

Bunce shook his head, breaking the memory into tiny pieces, reached for his trusty Maglite, and ran from his bedroom. He sprinted down the stairs, raced through the backdoor of the farmhouse, and set off across the fields after Pa. He moved briskly, knowing that he could walk safely in the Fade and not be seen. Pa might look back, but the Fade would protect him. It always did. It was like walking in a vast, empty space where the edges of the world became blurred. Bunce often retreated to the Fade whenever he felt threatened. There was nothing there that could hurt him. It was like stepping inside a wide shadow and allowing its subtle darkness to fill him with its message of relief. When he emerged, he moved in a vacuum, darkly attenuated, shifting in an unseen conjuration of air. Using the Fade was like passing into a fourth dimension, in which only Bunce was authorized to travel, rendering him unreachable, complicit; free.

He pressed on, following Pa without anxiety, confident that the Fade would conceal him. He could see the woods up ahead more clearly now, though the land around it was darkening fast. Pa was heading for a narrow opening between the trees and Bunce watched him remove a small torch from his pocket, turn on the beam, and disappear down a rough path of his own making. He followed the beam of light for a moment and then approached the same opening and pushed past the flailing arms of the trees. It was darker inside the woods and the ground was seamed with exposed roots. Bunce tried to navigate his way through the trees, following the wavering beam of Pa's torch, but the task was made trickier by the dark branches rising towards his face. He batted aimlessly at them, but felt them clawing at his face; their scratches reminded him of Fliss and her wild attack earlier in the day and he knew that yet more blood was being drawn for the cause. He scowled in the shadow of the dense trees and wondered how much he'd end up shedding before the day was done. Though the Fade could protect him from Pa, it clearly couldn't protect him from nature. The thought made him suddenly afraid.

He continued on through the woods, following Pa's torch. He tried to make as little noise as possible, but at one point he heard Pa stop and saw the beam of light pass close to where he was standing. He froze and nestled deeply into the pocket of the Fade. The beam closed in. Bunce held his breath, but the light passed over him and moved deeper into the nearby trees. A few seconds later, Pa moved on, the torchlight bouncing off the leaves. Bunce followed, picking his way along the barely-visible path, his dark profile concealed by the Fade. Pa's destination remained unclear, but Bunce was determined to see where he ended up. It wasn't just the wooden box that intrigued him, it was also the strange intensity of Pa's passage through the woods. He seemed to know exactly where he was going. He was powering towards a destination that he had clearly visited before, and Bunce was curious to find out what lay in the woods that had the power to lure Pa so far from the comfort of his home.

Father and son edged forward, easing through the thick growth of wild brambles and gorse, the man in front unaware of the pursuing shadow behind. Eventually, after an additional several hundred yards of wrestling through coarse woodland, Pa stumbled into an uneven clearing. It was dark enough to make Bunce squint through the trees, and he resisted the urge to turn on the Maglite. A narrow shaft of moonlight caught the side of Pa's face and showed Bunce a man in the grip of a fierce, unnamable emotion. Whatever Pa was doing here, it was leaving a lasting impression; there was evidence of a deep sorrow etched into the moonlit contours of his face.

Despite this, he appeared to know exactly what he was doing, as though the process of carrying it out had become commonplace. He moved towards the edge of the clearing, directed the beam of his torch towards a cluster of heavy rocks, and then stooped down beside them. Bunce watched as he placed Ma's jewelry box on the ground and then perched the torch on the wooden lid. He could see that Pa looked suddenly nervous, and he called himself deeper into the Fade as Pa performed a lengthy examination of the surrounding woods. When he was content that he was alone, he eased forward and, with considerable effort, lifted the largest rock from the cluster and moved it several feet to the side. Bunce smiled as the moonlight passed across a small hole in the ground. He had stumbled upon Pa's secret hiding place. The rock was nothing more than a decoy. A damn good one, too, Bunce thought. Pa could take his treasures and stash them away from prying eyes. It was the perfect place to store objects he didn't want Fliss to stumble upon, like Ma's jewelry box.

Pa retrieved the torch and shone the light into the hole. He made some space among the items that were already down there and then reached for the box. He took a Ziploc bag from his pocket, placed the box inside and secured the seal. Satisfied that the bag was airtight, he lowered the box into the hole. In no time at all he then returned the rock to its rightful position, rearranged the cluster so that it appeared untouched, and set off back through the woods.

Bunce watched fascinated as Pa performed his solemn ritual. There was something remarkably discomforting about the whole process, as though he were watching Pa through a slightly warped lens offering a distorted view of his father's behavior. Bunce waited for several minutes as Pa retreated through the woods, and tried to remember a time when he had ever seen his father behave so strangely. Nothing sprang to mind. During the minutes he spent waiting for Pa to return to the farmhouse, he considered what he might find inside the hole. The thought of reaching his arm into the darkness filled him with a wild mixture of exhilaration and shame. It would be like slipping his hand into Pa's soul. The thought made him feel wretched. Such an invasion seemed like a breach of intimacy and the idea suddenly repelled him. It was only when he remembered the jewelry box, and the other treasures that Pa might have stashed in the hole, that his determination to follow his plan through was revived.

After waiting a further few minutes to make sure Pa wasn't coming back, Bunce emerged from the safety of the Fade. He approached the cluster of rocks on the far side of the clearing and paused. He knelt down, removed his Maglite and turned it on. The beam was narrow and bright. He directed it at the large rock that he had seen his father dislodge. He placed the torch on the ground, lifted the rock and moved it away from the hole. He picked up the Maglite and shone it inside the dark space he had just exposed. His heart was racing. He felt like a kid again, primed for some grand discovery, the likes of which might very well shape the rest of his life.

He reached inside the hole and pulled out the jewelry box inside the Ziploc bag. He held his breath and stared at it for a moment in the erratic moonlight. He thought of his Ma, lost to them these past eight months, and silently drew open the zip. He removed the box and set it in the palm of his left hand. With his right, he held on to the torch and lifted the lid. He heard a familiar tune, as the musical cylinder was activated. He shone the torch inside and gasped.

The lining of the jewelry box contained a severed finger. Where it had been cut, white bone glinted in the light. A gold wedding band was still attached to it and Bunce found himself staring at it, mesmerized. He had seen it many times. The last time he had noticed it Ma had been wearing it as she'd kissed him on the cheek. Now, here it was, still wrapped around Ma's finger, buried in a hole in a box. A lost keepsake; a symbol of some greater horror. A perfectly preserved circle of guilt.

3

NEW HORIZON

Philip had been out of the hospital for over three weeks and had quickly reverted to his abnormal self. Dr. Crozier had allowed him to take home one of the NHS clipboards and a handful of blank medical charts. Father had been appalled. He accused Dr. Crozier of indulging Philip's ongoing obsession with his health, and chided him for giving away NHS property without first obtaining the appropriate authorization. When Father ran his mouth like this, Mother would invariably sigh and leave the room, having heard it all before.

"No use ignoring it, Cynth!" Father would shout after her. "It's why this country's going to the dogs! Misappropriation of public property!"

Mother would continue on up the stairs and begin folding laundry in one of the bedrooms. Anything to avoid listening to yet another of Father's half-baked, asinine rants.

Down below she would hear Philip pass into the living room, consult his chart and stand peering at his latest invented disease.

"Put down that damn clipboard!" Father would yell. "It's driving me nuts."

Philip would stare at him for a moment, as though noticing him for the first time, and then walk solemnly out of the room.

This scene, or something like it, was enacted two or three times every day. It was a painful reminder of the world they now inhabited; a world in which each member of the family felt lost, where only Philip, with his NHS clipboard, knew the code that let on to a new horizon.

———

As the days passed, Saul and Amy learnt to adjust to their brother's unpredictable behavior. While their parents continued to struggle vainly with the notion that Philip could be transformed into a normal child again, Saul and Amy began to accept him for who he was. They both grew less afraid of him and even started to engage in some of his milder delusions, much to Father's increasing horror.

He walked into Amy's bedroom one evening to find Saul lying on her bed, being attended to by Philip, with his NHS clipboard, and Amy, who had donned her nurse's outfit from her dressing-up box.

"What on earth is going on?" Father said.

"We're playing doctors and nurses," Amy said. "Like Philip does."

Father's face turned red with mounting frustration. "Saul," he said, in an attempt at patience. "Get off the bed. This kind of thing only encourages him. You should know that by now."

Saul sat up. "We want our brother back," he said. "This is the only way we can get close to him."

Father drew in a deep breath and stared at Philip, who was busy ticking off boxes on one of his charts.

"Philip, why don't you play something else? There are lots of games in the cupboard that you used to enjoy. Don't you remember?"

Philip shook his head without looking up. "No time for playing games. Too much to do. I still have another ward to attend to."

"There is no ward," Father said, exasperated. "Why don't you look around? See? You're at home, with Saul and Amy. You're playing a game."

Philip glanced up and looked at Father, who seemed on the edge of exhaustion. Saul could see dark shadows circling his eyes.

"Visiting hours are over," Philip said, and with that he promptly walked out of the room. They all listened to him walk down the stairs and exit the house by the back door.

Father stared at Saul and Amy and for a moment a look of desperate understanding passed between them. Then Father turned away and grunted.

"Take off that uniform," he said to Amy. "It looks ridiculous."

He left the room and quietly shut the door. Saul guessed he would spend the rest of the night drinking. Father's way of blotting out the world. No code for him, more like a sledgehammer; but it always seemed to get the job done.

Mother sat in her chair and watched the rain lash against the window. Another typical English day. She saw people scurrying down the street with umbrellas, their faces hidden by nylon hoods, and wondered what kind of life awaited them when they arrived home. She tried to remember what *her* old life had been like before Philip had fallen ill, but it seemed so long ago now that the memories barely registered as hers. It seemed like the life of a different woman completely, a more fearless woman, one in control of her own destiny, whose decision to get married and have a family must have made perfect sense at the time.

Now, here she sat feeling like a burst bubble. Whenever she wasn't chasing after Frank and the kids and had time to sit down, even for a minute, the depth of her fatigue overwhelmed her. She couldn't remember ever having felt this tired before, not even when the kids were young. Frank was more inclined to help out then, she recalled; that was the difference. He was not yet addicted to the sauce. Now, a night barely went by when her husband of nineteen years didn't immerse himself in the bottle and go in search of his own private redemption. She tried to remember when his drinking had passed from a can or two at night in front of the box, to the uncontrollable addiction that he now fought every day of every week of the year. She was ashamed to admit that the transition had somehow passed her by. She thought about it for a moment and closed her eyes, zeroing in on a shocking realization. In many ways, she had been complicit in the process. How many nights had she pulled back the tab on a can of lager and placed it on the kitchen table by his plate? How many times had she brought him another cold one fresh from the fridge, smiling as Frank patted her on the bottom, the beer loosening his tongue and gradually lightening his mood?

The idea was a chastening one, but it was hard to deny. She had unwittingly reinforced Frank's drinking habits and was now having to live with the consequences. She paused for a moment and thought. Had she really done so *unwittingly*? Or had she always known, right from the very start, how dangerous it was to mix liquor and love?

She closed her eyes again. It was difficult to consider any of this without shedding a tear or two and she really didn't feel like crying anymore. She had wept enough. Not just for Frank and their hopeless, loveless marriage, but for the kids, too. She had spent countless nights in this very chair, flicking through the bloated photograph album, crying silently to herself while her family slept on upstairs.

It all amounted to a simple, horrifying truth: this was her life. Knowing that she had been responsible for creating it caused a small part of her to shrivel up and die inside.

When Saul woke up the following morning, he glanced across the landing at Philip's bed and noticed that it was empty. It had already been neatly reassembled with the covers tucked between the mattress and the frame. Saul checked the clock on his bedside cabinet. It informed him that it was 8:23am. He rose, stretched, ran a hand through the morning chaos of his hair, and trudged over to the window. It was bright outside with a thin layer of frost on the grass. His bedroom looked onto the property's large back garden and he stood for a moment and stared at the scene before him.

Down below, moving slowly between the sunlit apple trees, was Philip. He was walking steadily, his eyes focused on the ground. Every so often, he paused, went down on one knee, and spent a moment inspecting the fallen leaves. Eventually, he would pick one up, hold it to his nose, take a deep breath, and then drop the chosen leaf into a small plastic tub.

Directly behind him, stumbling a little on the uneven terrain, was Amy. Saul watched her from the bedroom window and smiled. She was imitating every movement Philip made: choosing a leaf, inspecting it, sniffing it, and then finally dropping it into a plastic tub. She was watching Philip intently. Everything he did, she seemed determined to duplicate, shadowing Philip with a fierce resolve that Saul could only stand and admire.

He wondered what the leaves might be for, but very quickly reminded himself that, where Philip was concerned, logical questions such as this simply didn't apply. In Philip's mind the question would never be: *Why am I collecting leaves?* The notion would merely settle in his brain as an imperative: *I have to collect leaves.* Why that might be would never be an issue, not for Philip. It was the kind of thing that might drive Father crazy; the not knowing; the pointlessness of it all. But for Philip, the collecting was enough. It didn't have to possess any kind of internal logic. Philip's world was structured differently. The things he did couldn't be measured; it would be futile to even try.

Saul considered all this for a moment and decided that there was a kind of weird dignity in passing through life with such an uncomplicated world view. Philip drifted through life without any safety net, an idea that Saul found utterly terrifying. Was he even aware of how dangerous the universe could be?

He watched his brother walk through the garden in the early morning sunlight, picking up leaves and placing them in a tub. Five steps behind, his sister did exactly the same, unaware of why she was doing it, just delighting in that sense of being free.

Saul got dressed and, while Philip was still preoccupied collecting leaves, decided to pay a visit to their neighbor, Bernard Putts. He entered through the man's yard and approached his workshop at the back of the house. He could see Bernard sanding down an old rocking chair, taking his time, refusing to be rushed, doing the job exactly as he knew it should be done. He looked up as Saul's shadow fell across the porch.

"Morning," he said, smiling. "Don't often get to see you round here, Saul. I was expecting your brother. He usually brings me a cup of tea round about this time."

Saul stepped into the workshop, frowning.

"Philip brings you tea?"

It was difficult to believe; it sounded too *normal* for a start. It was exactly the kind of courtesy Philip would have resisted. Correction: he wouldn't even be conscious of such a thing. That was more like it, Saul thought.

Bernard nodded. "Most mornings. He tells me he makes it himself, but I've a suspicion your dear mother might lend a hand."

Saul considered this and thought it unlikely. He checked his watch. It was 8:48am. Mother never even surfaced until at least nine o'clock. She told all of them it was an unwritten rule.

"He's collecting leaves," Saul said. "Maybe he'll be over later."

Bernard nodded, as though the news that Philip was gathering leaves was the most sensible announcement he had heard all day.

"Don't you want to know why he's collecting them?" Saul said.

Bernard stopped sanding the rocking chair and looked at him. "Is it important I know?"

Saul looked confused. The question had thrown him, though the more he thought about it, the more it seemed to explain why Bernard and Philip had become friends.

"I don't know why he's collecting them," Saul said finally. "No one does. Probably not even Philip."

Bernard smiled and began sanding the chair again.

"That's alright," he said. "Perhaps he's doing it for the same reason that I'm sanding this chair."

Saul frowned. "But that's your job."

"That may be so," Bernard said. "But it also clears the mind and gets the blood flowing. A perfect way to start the day, wouldn't you agree?"

Saul nodded, and was shocked to discover that he was envious of Philip's friendship with this man. It was a strange feeling; he couldn't remember ever being envious of anything Philip possessed. It made him feel slightly light-headed.

"Would you like *me* to fetch you a cup of tea?" Saul suddenly suggested.

Bernard shook his head. "I don't think Philip would like that. Do you?"

Saul felt his face grow hot and cursed his foolishness. He was ashamed that he had even proposed making the tea. It made him seem petty and small; a bad brother, too eager to take advantage of Philip's oversights. Bernard wasn't the kind of man who would fail to notice such things. He looked across at him and realized that Bernard was staring back; his gaze looked cool and analytical, as though he was judging Saul with disapproving eyes. He seemed to be waiting to see what the boy would say next.

"You look busy," he said, trying to shift the conversation away from his brother.

Bernard nodded and continued sanding. "That's the secret," he said, smiling. "Always *look* busy, even when you're not." He paused for a moment, then added: "It sounds like Philip understands this trick, too." He shook his head and laughed, then muttered under his breath, "Leaves..."

Saul felt like he'd missed something. He played the conversation back in his head while Bernard attended to the chair, but, if there was a mystery locked inside Bernard's words, it was too cryptic for Saul to decode.

Instead, he padded around the workshop, caressing dull wooden instruments that in Bernard's hands seemed to spring to life and produce objects of beauty, some of which were displayed on cluttered benches and shelves.

"Do you like making things?" Saul asked. He was running his hand across the smooth plane of a carved elephant's head. The tusks and the trunk felt so lifelike, he closed his eyes and briefly imagined himself transported to a faraway land.

"What's not to like? In here it's just me and the wood. The rest of the world might just as well not exist." He paused for a moment and then said, "Listen. Can you hear that?"

Saul concentrated for a moment before finally shaking his head. "I don't hear anything."

Bernard looked disappointed. "What you hear is silence. There's not even the sound of a ticking clock. When I work, I hear everything the wood has to say to me. Not a beat is missed. Do you understand that, Saul? Do you see how important that is to a man like me?"

Saul was desperate to grasp the significance of what Bernard was saying, but much of it seemed like it was meant for someone else, as though he was addressing a hidden part of himself as much as he was confiding in Saul. Still, he nodded, eager not to appear ignorant of the man's observation. He wanted to understand; he wanted to appreciate Bernard's unusual train of thought.

"I like silence too," he said, and instantly regretted offering such a bland statement.

He saw Bernard's eyes subtly shift and heard him emit a deep sigh.

"You talk a lot," he said. "Much more than Philip. Sometimes, he's so quiet I don't even know he's here."

He picked up the sanding block and silently began working on the chair.

Picking up on his cue, Saul turned away. He felt deflated, as though he'd squandered an opportunity. He walked back through the workshop and stopped just before he reached the door. On a nearby worktop was a sheet of A3 paper, bearing a picture of a flat, shaded terrain. In the middle of the page was a small boy; he was surrounded by grey, empty space. In the distance there was the suggestion of hills and a windless shore.

"What's this?" Saul said, pointing to the image.

Bernard glanced up and smiled. "Your brother did it," he said. "Spent ages on it, too. Told me it's the place he sometimes visits when he needs to be alone. He calls it The Fade."

Bernard returned to his work and Saul stared at the picture, admiring the depth of the shading, the artistry of the textured landscape Philip had depicted. The Fade. Saul smiled, liking the sound of the name. He briefly considered what other wonders existed inside his brother's head, and left Bernard's workshop deciding he may have stumbled upon a secret after all.

Later that afternoon, as Father returned from his shift, Saul heard a wail of distress coming from the kitchen. He rushed from his room and ran down the stairs. Father still had his coat on. He was standing in the middle of the kitchen, staring at the far wall. His face was a picture of horror and outrage. Behind him, Saul could see Philip in his white doctor's coat. He was jittery with motion. He held his plastic tub in one hand and a pot of glue in the other.

"For the love of God," he heard Father say. "Cynth! *CYNTH!* Get the hell in here. He's gluing leaves all over the kitchen wall!" His face started to turn puce and Saul held a hand over his mouth. "*Leaves!*" Father shouted at the top of his voice.

Mother came running into the kitchen and stood next to Father, staring at Philip's handiwork. From where Saul stood at the bottom of the stairs he had a good view of the wall, which was now decorated with dozens of leaves. The autumnal reds and browns and yellows looked beautiful, he thought, but Father clearly didn't agree.

Mother took a tentative step towards Philip and held out her hand towards him. It rested gently on his arm. Philip turned to look at her, waiting.

"What are you doing, sweetheart?"

Philip frowned, as though it were obvious.

"I'm bringing them back to life," he said. "They can live here forever."

Father turned away, exasperated, muttering something under his breath. Mother ignored him and reached for the pot of glue.

"Let's have a rest," she said. "Perhaps we can talk about it some more in the morning. Okay?"

Philip allowed her to take the pot of glue and the tub of leaves from his hands and the pair of them walked past Father and disappeared upstairs.

Saul kept his eyes on Father, who was still staring in disbelief at the wall of leaves.

"Is this what it's come to?" he shouted after Mother and Philip. "We indulge every act of craziness now? Every bloody insanity that he acts out? Maybe we should all do that. What do you think, Saul? Perhaps we should all do whatever the hell we please." He started leaping around the kitchen, throwing some of the crockery from the sink and smashing it on the floor. "Look. I'm making the plates dance! They're alive, Saul! *They're alive!* Come on, son. Don't just stand there. If we work together we can bring the rest of the fucking house to life."

He stopped then and held his head in his hands, staring at Saul. He was breathing hard; a wing of jet black hair had fallen across his brow. He looked desperately ashamed of himself. Saul glanced around the kitchen floor at the mess his father had created and then turned and walked away. Father stood in the silence of the kitchen, watching his son disappear. He stared at the leaves glued to the wall. He closed his eyes, tried to remember when life had become so tiring, so hollow; why he felt such a profound emptiness inside.

Saul decided to go in search of Amy, primarily to ensure that she steered well clear of the house while something was running loose in Father's head. He found her near the bottom of the garden. She was bent over, staring at something on the ground. She had a toy magnifying glass in her hand.

"Found anything exciting?" Saul asked.

Amy turned her head towards him and gave a jolt. There was a confused expression on her face that teetered between pity and pain. For a moment Saul thought his sister was going to cry. Instead, she pointed at the ground and took a step back, allowing Saul to see what was lying in the grass. He stooped down for a closer look and saw a baby bird, featherless and pink with a tiny yellow beak. It was dead, Saul realized, probably from stumbling blindly out of its nest. He was glad Philip hadn't been the one to find it. He would have spent the rest of the day trying to resurrect it. *That's what doctors do*, he could hear Philip insisting. *They heal things*. Saul could imagine Philip waving his clipboard in his face and starting a new chart for the bird. He would have dedicated himself to saving the poor creature's soul.

"What is it?" Amy said, peering at it. She wore a look of distaste, as though the reality of death daring to venture so close, in her own garden, no less, was a personal affront. She wore an expression that reminded Saul so much of Mother's moral indignation it was frightening.

"It's a nestling," Saul said.

Amy looked up at him, accepting this new word but failing to understand.

"A baby bird that hasn't left the nest yet."

Amy nodded and stared back down at the tiny pink body. "What happened to it?"

"Looks like it tried to fly too soon," Saul said. "The silly thing must have got too close to the edge. Or else thought it was strong enough to leave home. Either way, the result's the same, isn't it?"

Amy said nothing. She held the magnifying glass up to her face and bent towards the grass. Saul could see the enlarged head of the dead bird through the lens.

"We need to bury it," she said. "That's the right thing to do."

Saul smiled and shook his head. "Not on this occasion, kiddo. Sometimes nature gets what's left. Unfortunately, this little critter's fate is to feed whatever hungry predator comes along first. That's how the whole system works, I'm afraid."

Amy grimaced and looked indignant. "But some nasty cat will eat it," she said. "That's what'll happen."

Saul smiled again and found it hard to argue with his sister's bleak world view. "Not always," he said. "And anyway, that's not for us to decide. We're not God, Amy. What will be will be, right?"

She glanced up and nodded, though Saul thought the gesture lacked conviction. She wanted to intercede, he could sense that; wanted to make sure that the body of the idiot bird was at rest.

He braced himself for a fresh wave of questions when he caught sight of Philip wandering in one of the distant fields beyond the fence. He stepped across the muddy verge at the bottom of the garden and clambered up the angled concrete post. He hung onto the fence and watched as Philip trudged across the field. It was like watching an old film, where the picture kept flickering in and out of focus. Saul frowned and blinked his eyes. They were watering badly as though he were staring at the sun, and he repeatedly turned away, then turned back, hoping that his impaired vision would eventually be restored.

"What is it?" Amy said. "Let me see."

Saul waved a hand to quieten her and tried instead to focus on Philip as he strode across the open field. He seemed to be wavering, flickering, like a child's poorly animated cartoon. Saul frowned again, trying to understand what his eyes were showing him; a vision where the rest of the landscape was laid out in perfect sunlit clarity, but where his brother grew increasingly vague, until he passed from dim to hazy to indistinct and then faded from view altogether, leaving behind a soft fluttering veil of empty space.

4

A HAPPY PLACE

Bunce pulled the van into its customary spot opposite the vicarage and turned on the chimes. He sat for a moment, thinking. He was still trying to process the previous night's discovery. As well as Ma's wedding ring finger, he had found a number of other keepsakes inside the box Pa had buried: a few old photos, a poorly-composed poem, a seashell and a lace handkerchief bearing Ma's initials. It was like stumbling upon a time-bomb, one that had carelessly exploded in Bunce's face, leaving him with a broken heart and a terror of returning home. His discovery had turned him ice cold and, in a state of uncomprehending shock, his hands still trembling badly, he had returned the box to the earth, and carefully replaced the rock. When he eventually found his way home he had spent the night in the Fade. He had walked miles across the flat emptiness of his private kingdom. He had wept for a long time, remembering the severed finger in the box.

He looked through the wide windscreen of the van and took a deep breath. It wasn't as warm today, but there'd be the usual steady flow of needy kids desperate for yet another sugar rush.

There always was. It was like in that film, he thought, smiling, the one with the flying car. The ice cream van was just like the child catcher's wagon; turn on the chimes and watch the kiddie-winks come running. It was fool-proof, Bunce thought. Those damn chimes brought the children rushing to his door every time.

He rose from the driver's seat and moved across the van to the large hatch through which he served. He smiled again; he could see half a dozen children racing down the road towards the van. They looked eager and impatient, almost grimacing as they ran, and for a moment he felt a dart of fear as they approached, their glassy eyes fixed on the colorful invitations that had been spray-painted all over the vehicle with the express purpose of drawing children to its door. He tried to put himself in their shoes and felt the sudden thrill of easy running and carefree living, their biggest worry of the day which ice cream they ought to choose. There was a large circular logo on the side of the van that depicted three grinning children, all wearing different colored blobs of ice cream for hair. There was a rainbow above them and the tag line *Ice Cream Makes The World A Happy Place*. For Bunce the statement had never seemed more true, nor more trite. He pulled open the window and gamely forced a smile onto his rueful face.

The first of the children reached the van and thrust a handful of coins towards him.

"What would you like, Sweetie?"

The girl looked up at him, seemingly puzzled by his stupidity.

"Ice cream," she said, and Bunce was unable to stop himself from mentally adding: *…you scream, we all scream for ice cream.* He stared down at her blank, emotionless face and felt a trickle of sweat bead down from his brow to his neck. He was conscious of the other kids watching him, waiting for him to reach for a cone. He glanced down at the girl again and tried to smile.

"Get a move on, Fatso, we haven't got all day."

Some of the other kids began to chuckle, and he looked up to see two larger boys at the back of the queue, grinning and waiting to see if he'd react.

"I have a strict policy," Bunce said. "Rude boys and girls won't get served. It's the Ice Cream Man's code."

He smiled out at the waiting children, praying that they wouldn't detect his sudden anxiety.

"Fuck the code," one of the boys said, and there was a large gasp from the other kids and stifled laughter.

Bunce ran his gaze over the two large boys and held his breath. They were older than the other kids, probably by five or six years. They were staring at him with a mixture of provocation and disgust. Their faces were pale and unlined, their eyes brimming with pent-up violence. Bunce could see them composing their next insult, a sly curling of the lip suggesting it was all too easy, given the obvious deficiencies of their prey.

Bunce turned back to the girl who'd asked for ice cream and wiped his brow with the back of his hand. It came away drenched in sweat and he could feel his cheeks burning, the back of his neck flushed with shame. He reached for a cone and positioned it beneath the ice cream dispenser. He filled it, added raspberry sauce, and handed it down to the girl.

"There you go, Sweetie," he said. He took the money from her greasy hand and forced one last smile onto features that felt painfully tight.

"Hey, you're not supposed to touch her like that," one of the boys shouted. "Fucking pervert."

His accomplice nodded and the two of them grinned and high-fived one another. Bunce stared at the boy who had spoken and noticed that he was wearing a shiny silver pin through his eyebrow. Bunce couldn't imagine for the life of him why the boy might do such a thing; it seemed utterly without meaning, a gesture designed to say nothing to anyone about anything. He found himself smiling, almost despite himself, and when he next looked up the boy with the pin was staring angrily at him.

"That what you are, mister? A fucking pervert who likes touching up little girls? My dad warned me about blokes like you."

The other children had started to disperse, sensing impending trouble, and Bunce noticed that the girl he had served had dropped her ice cream and was now running away crying down the road. He felt his heart start to race; felt a dark pounding deep inside his skull.

"This is how you talk to your elders?" he said. "I've a good mind to pay a visit to your parents, let them know exactly what they've brought into the world."

"You do that, mister," Silver Pin said. "My dad'll knock your fucking teeth out."

He snarled at Bunce and spat at him through the window as his friend stood beside him forcing fresh gales of laughter, as though exhausted by his companion's unpleasantness. Bunce wiped away the phlegm that had landed across his face and then wiped his hands down his apron, smearing the boy's malice across the suspended astronaut (*In space no one can eat ice cream*). The muscles in the back of his neck had turned to rocks and it felt like a lead weight had settled across his chest. He was dangerously close to disappearing into the Fade, which had become his automatic response to situations like this. It was as much as he could do to squeeze his fists together and hold the transition in check. He closed his eyes and blinked away thoughts of his safe place, breathing heavily.

"Hey, look," he heard Silver Pin say. "He's got his eyes closed. Bet he's got you trapped in that sick head of his, Vic, all naked and that. Dirty bastard."

He listened to the boy's laughter as he tried to control his breathing. He thought they sounded like animals, snorting and braying, their malice reduced to a coil of sound that penetrated Bunce's throbbing skull.

He opened his eyes and the two boys stared at him with open hostility.

"We don't like kiddie-fiddlers," Silver Pin said. "Come round here again and you'll get what's coming to you. Fat cunts always do."

With that, the two boys turned on their heels and calmly walked away. Silver Pin's accomplice glanced over his shoulder once, wearing an expression of conflicted wonder, and then the pair turned the corner at the end of the street. Bunce released a long sigh and held a hand to his aching head. He felt drained. He closed the serving hatch and returned to the driver's seat of the van. He strapped himself in and drove away. One thought kept recurring and played on a loop inside his mind as he tried to erase the truculent faces of the two boys: *Ice Cream Makes The World A Happy Place.*

Back home, he parked the van in the barn and stepped through the stone archway to Pa's workshop. Gilly was seated at the long table, polishing his combat boots. Bunce paused and watched him at work. The Winchester Black Shadow was propped against the table beside him; as usual, he was dressed in full woodland ACU, which Gilly had told him stood for army combat uniform. Bunce also knew that his brother was polishing a pair of Grafters British assault boots. Gilly said it was called bulling, and he could sit for hours working on each boot until the leather shone like black glass.

"Where's Pa?" Bunce said, removing his apron and bundling it up on the worktop. He remembered wiping Silver Pin's phlegm down the front of it and almost gagged at the memory.

Gilly glanced up and noticed he had company. He looked back down at the boots, continued polishing, and flicked his head towards the door, indicating the farmhouse beyond the workshop.

"Him and Fliss are arguing," he said. "Best to take cover."

Bunce nodded. The last thing he wanted to do after last night's discovery was run into Pa. If he was arguing with Fliss, that would only make the whole situation even worse. He pulled up a stool and sat several feet away from Gilly, watching him work.

"You need a hand?" he said.

Gilly paused and stared at him. He held up the boots. "No one touches the black Cadillacs but me. You know the rules."

Another nod from Bunce. He did indeed know the rules; he had grown up listening to them. Gilly had marched to the same insane drum ever since he was a young kid. Bunce had watched him change from a boy with a dream to a man trapped inside a cruel delusion. Gilly was no more a soldier than Pa or Fliss, but in his head, where the darkness was always slippery, he could be anything he wanted to be. Bunce watched his brother polishing his boots and felt a momentary flood of grief at what his family had lost. He remembered how Ma would hold Gilly's hand whenever he grew upset, waiting until the anger and the resentment disappeared, cradling his face, talking to him softly while he wept. He'd had a chance back then, when Ma was still alive. They all had. Now, with Fliss and Pa fighting and Gilly polishing his assault boots, they were all doomed; every one of them. Bunce listened to the steady rhythm of Gilly's brush and felt like screaming into the face of his own destiny. He knew what was coming; he could sense it. Pa's secret was like a black mass boiling inside his skull, and Bunce could smell spilled blood and gun oil waiting for him in the haze up ahead.

Bunce entered the farmhouse by the back door and listened for voices. Other than the slow ticking of the kitchen clock and the hum of the refrigerator, the house was silent. Pa and Fliss had either drained themselves of anger and were recharging, or they had retired to separate parts of the house to lick their wounds. Either way, Bunce would have time to climb the stairs and lock himself inside his room. To be on the safe side, he eased into the cool anonymity of the Fade and waited until the white expanse of resettled air closed around him.

He passed through the utility room and the kitchen and moved silently down the blurred channel of the hall.

"It's like you want something to happen," he suddenly heard Fliss say. "Like you're waiting for the whole thing to collapse. Is that what it is?"

Bunce froze. Fliss's petulant voice was coming from the front room, no more than half a dozen steps to the right. The clipped tone and the dripping contempt were horribly familiar. The sound of it filled Bunce with dread.

"You're being irrational," Pa said. "That's the very last thing I want." There was a lengthy pause, before Pa continued. "I have my own reasons for going, Fliss. That's the truth of it. You're just going to have to accept that and deal with it the best you can."

Bunce heard a thudding of feet and imagined Fliss flying across the room until her face was pressed up against Pa's.

"*Don't you dare tell me what to do! Not ever. You slip up with your foolishness and we both suffer. Do you understand?*"

There was a moment's silence; Bunce pictured Fliss breathing heavily in Pa's arms.

"There'll be no more suffering," he said softly.

Bunce heard more noises, then retreating footsteps, and realized that Pa and Fliss were using the south door to pass into the kitchen. He seized his advantage and stole down the hall and up the stairs towards his room, still carried safely in the belly of the Fade.

The house fell silent again.

———————

Bunce lay on his bed with his eyes closed, staring at the dark. His room was small and unadorned, boasting only the bed on which he lay, a wardrobe, a desk and a small nightstand. He could picture it easily in his mind. This was his home; this was where he felt perfectly at peace. Even when Ma had been around, he had spent a lot of time up here. The simplicity of it helped him think. There were no distractions other than those he created in his own head.

This was proving useful now as he remembered Pa striding purposefully across the field toward the woods. He recalled the grisly shrine that Pa had created beneath the rock, Ma's jewelry box buried under the black earth containing the powerful mementoes: the poem; the seashell; the lace handkerchief. And most appalling of all, the severed finger bearing Ma's gold wedding band, nestled against the lining of the box.

He squeezed his eyes together to try and block out the image and felt his hands clench into fists by his side. It felt like he had too much information, none of which made any sense to him. Bunce was an uncomplicated man, who knew his own limitations. He wasn't good at solving puzzles or dragging his brain across life's profundities. He was good at dispensing ice cream and knowing when he should enter the Fade. These were his strengths, and Bunce rarely extended himself beyond what he knew.

But now, suddenly, there was this: a whole new situation, and one it was impossible for Bunce to ignore. This time the pieces of the puzzle had fallen into place almost before his very eyes. Even a simpleton like him could understand; he had seen and heard too much.

You slip up with your foolishness and we both suffer.

This is what Fliss had said to Pa. He replayed the comment in his head and listened to the squeal of resistance that was echoing off the walls of his skull. No matter how much he wished he hadn't heard it, the plain fact of the matter was, he had caught the words all too clearly; more alarmingly, he thought he knew exactly what they meant.

Bunce began to breathe heavily and pressed his fingers against his eyes. He could feel a nascent migraine back there, and the memory of Fliss's voice was like a spike being hammered into his brain.

It's like you want something to happen...Like you're waiting for the whole thing to collapse.

Bunce reeled at the memory. Fliss had been accusing Pa of putting the entire enterprise at risk. Did she know about Pa's trip to the woods, about the jewelry box buried beneath the rock? Bunce thought not. But she suspected something, that was for sure, and she was afraid that Pa's grief would lead to him confessing to whatever terrible thing they had inflicted on Ma.

Bunce finally opened his eyes. He felt like a man wandering in a dream. He felt dispossessed and lonely; he realized he missed his mother more than he had the capacity to understand. He stared at the prominent veins climbing the underside of his forearm below the wrist and wondered why they were a dark, shadowy blue. It was another riddle his simple brain would never be able to assimilate. Instead, he pictured the red blood racing up his arm towards his heart.

Blood, he thought. *There had been blood.* This was what he focused on as he lay on the bed and listened to the silence of the house. What had Pa done? What horror had that awful woman seduced him into? He pictured Ma's tired, smiling face, then the severed finger and the ring. Finally, he closed his eyes again, and wept. He stayed that way until the room and the sky outside turned dark.

Later that night Bunce was jarred awake by a noise out in the barn, which was followed by a lingering silence. He rubbed his eyes and glanced at the clock on the nightstand; it read 00.25am. He raised himself on one elbow and shook the remnants of a dream from his head. He listened, frowning, anticipating a recurrence of the noise. He suspected Gilly of leaving the barn door ajar and was convinced the noise had been made by a predator rummaging for food, probably a fox or a damn badger.

He clambered out of bed and reached for the clothes he had strewn across the floor. A fragment of the dream had stayed with him, loosely scrambled in his brain, and he pictured the large boy with the silver pin in his eyebrow wearing the face of a fox, grinning at him and displaying a row of impossibly sharp teeth.

He shook his head again and stumbled towards the window. He drew back one of the curtains and peered down into the dimly-lit yard. If he expected to see signs of an intruder, he was disappointed. The porch light showed nothing but an emphatic darkness. He peered hard at it for a moment before finally accepting that the cobbled yard was deserted.

He would have to go down. The door of the barn was just out of sight, but he knew he'd be unable to sleep unless he checked it. He cursed Gilly under his breath and slipped into his shoes. So much for his brother's meticulous combat skills; he'd been so fixated on polishing his bloody boots, he'd forgotten to bolt the door.

Bunce left his room and quietly descended the stairs. The temperature had dropped and he could see ghostly plumes of breath like empty speech bubbles curling away from his mouth. He reached the bottom of the stairs, walked down the hall, and headed for the utility room. He turned on the light and paused for a moment, thinking. The silence of the house felt like a slow build-up of pressure, as though the whole place was waiting for him to make a mistake. He held his breath, barely conscious of having done so, and lifted a high powered Coleman torch from the shelf. He flicked it on and felt a little steadier for wielding its light. The beam was like a car's headlight; the darkness had little choice but to retreat. He unlocked the back door, opened it, and, guided by the harsh glare of the torch, walked across the yard towards the barn.

He knew immediately that something was not quite right. The barn door was ajar, as he'd suspected, but the main light was on, too. Had Gilly been foolish enough to leave the light burning when he left the barn?

He approached the door and raised the torch, prepared to use it like a club should the intruder be waiting for him just inside the barn. It never occurred to him once to enter the Fade, which, when he thought about it all later, seemed to suggest that he never really considered himself in any danger. Why that might be he couldn't quite determine, but a hollow darkness lay at the core of Bunce's deliberation that made him feel uneasy. A voice at the back of his head whispered to him that he already knew who was lurking in the barn: *It's the fox and the badger; the badger and the fox. They have a silver pin pushed through the fur above their eye and their teeth are impossibly sharp.*

He dislodged the thought with a vigorous shake of the head, passed beneath the frame of the door, and saw Fliss and Gilly staring at him from the opposite side of the barn. Gilly was pointing the barrel of the Winchester Black Shadow directly at his heart; Fliss was smoking a cigarette. They both appeared perfectly calm.

Bunce frowned, unable to process what he was seeing.

"I thought we had intruders," he said, feeling slightly dazed.

Fliss hesitated. "So did we. I guess we must have heard the same noise you did."

Gilly was staring at Bunce with a kind of abstract disdain, as though he wasn't even worthy of that. His eyes were dark and unblinking. Bunce ignored him; he was trying to remember if he'd heard any noises in the house, if it were at all possible for Gilly and Fliss to reach the barn without him having seen them cross the yard.

"How about you lower that damn gun," he said finally, tiring of Gilly's truculent stare. "I've seen you with that thing; you're like a maniac."

Gilly lowered the Winchester, but continued to stare at Bunce.

"You shouldn't be here," he said. "It might be dangerous."

Bunce nodded towards Fliss. "She's here," he said. He looked at Fliss as she smoked the cigarette and noticed for the first time that she was fully dressed. Both of them were. They hadn't grabbed the clothes nearest to hand and flung them on, as Bunce had. They were fully attired. Gilly had on his freshly-polished Grafters assault boots, Bunce noticed; he had even found the time to lace them.

"She's with me," Gilly said flatly.

Fliss smiled and exhaled a long contrail of smoke.

"Whatever made the noise must have escaped," she said. "There's nothing in the barn. Gilly and I have already checked."

Bunce frowned again, finding it difficult to imagine such a thing possible. They could only have been in the barn a fraction longer than Bunce himself.

"Perhaps you missed something. Why don't we look again? It might save us having to get up later in the night."

Gilly made a noise deep in the back of his throat and adjusted the rifle on his arm.

"Bollocks to that," he said. "There's nothing here, Hilary. Trust me. Fliss and I have already looked. It's time to sack out."

Bunce paused. "Maybe I'll just give it one more—"

Gilly placed his hand on Bunce's arm and looked him in the eye. "Stand down, soldier. This place has been swept clean."

He displayed a humorless smile and Bunce realized that his brother would indulge no defiance on the matter. As far as Gilly was concerned, the situation had been dealt with; it was time to retire for the night.

Bunce glanced around the barn, feeling like he was missing something. He listened for a repeat of the noise he had heard up in his room, but heard only the sound of his own breathing and the satisfied sigh of Fliss exhaling smoke. He looked across at her and she stared back at him, her gaze like the measured movement of a blade. For a moment, neither of them looked away, then Bunce averted his eyes and found himself staring at the ground beneath his feet.

When he next looked up, Gilly was turning out the barn light. He waited for Bunce and Fliss to join him in the yard and then made a point of locking the door with Pa's key. Without another word, Fliss and Gilly disappeared inside the house. Bunce stood alone in the dark. He thought about the badger and the fox; he remembered the sharp teeth of his dream. *Something's coming*, he thought; *something terrible*. He could feel it in the marrow of his bones.

Bunce had driven around in the van for a week looking for Silver Pin, but it was only on the seventh day that he finally found him. He was wearing the same faded black jacket and distressed trainers, but this time he was travelling alone. His hands were buried in the pockets of his jeans and a black hood covered his head. From the waist up, he looked to Bunce like an abbot wearing a cowl; he couldn't fathom for a second why the boy would want to appropriate such an effect. He imagined Silver Pin kneeling before his god, and wondered what depraved deity would ever embrace a child with so much bile in his heart.

He guided the van fifty yards beyond the boy and pulled up to the curb. He checked the wing mirror and saw Silver Pin start to slow down as it dawned on him that the fat ice cream man was waiting inside. He watched as the boy began to smile and felt a knot of tension in his chest. He released the seatbelt, deliberately chose not to engage the chimes, and opened the serving hatch in the side of the van.

The boy inched closer and his smile turned into a sneer. "I thought I told you not to come round here no more," he said. "Weren't you listening?"

Bunce took a deep breath and wiped a ring of sweat from his face. He felt a dull ache just behind his left eye; by this evening his head would be pounding. He placed a hand against his temple and pressed hard in a vain attempt to drive away the discomfort. He couldn't afford to lose focus. He was here to do a job. There was no room for error no matter how unforgiving the pain.

He peered out of the hatch and looked up and down the street; other than him and the boy it was more or less empty. In the distance, a woman was walking in the opposite direction pushing a pram. He could hear a dog barking in the nearby woods. Somewhere a small child was crying.

He returned his attention to the boy and tried to imagine what his parents must be like, what his teachers thought of him, how many children he terrorized as they passed into his orbit at school. He looked fairly normal, Bunce thought; just another kid with a grudge against the world. He stared at the silver pin lodged in his eyebrow, mesmerized by it. He watched the dark eyes stare back, judging him, full of anger and hate. He wondered if the boy had any idea why he was feeling that way.

"I had to come back," Bunce said. "I wanted to see you. I've been thinking about you a lot. I can't seem to get you out of my head."

Silver Pin's face crumpled in disgust. He looked like he had just been winded. For a moment he seemed almost lost for words.

"I was right," he said, jabbing a finger in Bunce's direction. "You really are a sick bastard. I knew you were a fucking pervert the minute I saw you."

Bunce smiled. "That's not it," he said. He pulled a cone from the rack and held it under the ice cream dispenser. "That's not it at all."

Silver Pin was snarling now, his body animated with angry tics. He took a phone from his pocket and held it up.

"You need to go right now, mister. I mean it. No more games."

Bunce finished preparing the cone, added a squirt of raspberry sauce, and held it out to the boy through the hatch. He smiled.

"Why don't you take this instead? You might like it."

Silver Pin looked aghast; his face turned red with unexpressed rage.

"I ain't taking no ice cream off you, you fucking weirdo. Take it back."

Bunce left his hand extended, holding out the cone. "It's just an ice cream," he said, still smiling. "What's so terrible about that?"

He kept his eye on the boy as he stared at the cone and realized that a bead of ice cream had already started to dribble down his hand.

The boy suddenly rushed at him and yelled, "*Take the fucking thing back! I don't want it! I don't want anything from you. Not a single fucking thing!"*

He lunged at Bunce and shoved the ice cream cone into his belly, where it spread across his apron in a milky explosion, smearing the astronaut and his humorous message (*In space no one can eat ice cream*) with broken bits of wafer and raspberry sauce. Bunce released a heavy whoosh of air as the boy barreled into him and then braced his feet against the floor of the van. He wrapped his large hands around Silver Pin's head and the difference in size between them became immediately apparent. Bunce was reminded that this was just a miserable kid, not a monster as he'd previously imagined. Nothing more than a young boy, railing against a universe he didn't understand. He was still bellowing and screaming insults at him, but Bunce's hands enveloped his skull with frightening ease and dragged him through the serving hatch of the van. The boy was kicking now and scrambling to recover his feet. He knew he was in trouble and was flailing wildly at Bunce, trying to unbalance him, attempting to turn and launch himself back beyond his assailant's embrace through the hatch. Bunce smiled, comforted by the boy's sudden recognition of his plight. He released Silver Pin's head and reached for the ice cream scoop. He looked the boy in the eye; unflinching terror stared back. It was perfect. Bunce raised the metal scoop in the air and brought it down quickly across the boy's skull. The van fell silent. Bunce stood for a moment, unmoving. It had all been remarkably easy, like setting in motion a machine. For the first time he actually felt pleased with himself. He had done what needed to be done.

He retrieved a ball of twine from behind the wheel arch, tied the boy's hands and feet, and stuffed a dry rag inside his mouth. Seconds later, the ice cream van, ponderous and unnoticed, pulled away from the side of the road.

5

DISTANT SHORE

Saul knocked on the door, took a step back, and waited. The rest of the house was quiet; Amy was out playing with a friend, and Father was downstairs reading yesterday's newspaper. Mother had gone to the shops, though Saul thought she had been gone an awfully long time. He suspected she often took the long route home. There was, after all, very little to rush back to; just a house full of awkward silences and frayed edges, a family struggling to rediscover its soul.

He knocked again, this time a little harder, and Philip's reedy voice beyond the door said: "Enter."

Saul did as instructed and saw Philip seated at his desk, picking apart the mechanism of an old clock.

"What are you doing?" he said.

Philip sighed and turned away from his task. Saul noticed he was holding a pair of tweezers in one hand and a tiny bradawl in the other. He recognized both items instantly; they had been taken from Saul's craft set. Mother would blow a gasket if she knew what Philip was meddling with. There were certain things in the house that he simply wasn't allowed to touch. Saul guessed that these basic art tools would be top of the list.

"This is where time lives," Philip explained impatiently. "Inside the clocks. If you're careful, you can control it. You can stop it from moving forward. Sometimes you can even reverse it."

Saul nodded politely, having learnt a long time ago to agree unconditionally with Philip's more eccentric ideas. Opposition only ever led to tantrums and turmoil; it was easier to simply nod your head and move on.

"It's the cogs, see? These tiny wheels. They're all connected somehow. They keep time ticking over. That's where it hides. In there."

He sounded alarmingly convincing and Saul listened to his crazy logic like an acolyte desperate to attend to his master's needs.

"Do you like mysteries, Saul?"

The question was unexpected and when Saul looked up from the disassembled clock he saw that Philip was staring at him. His eyes were half-closed, as though edging towards a dream, but he was waiting for an answer, the bradawl and the tweezers poised above the loose components of the clock.

"What kind of mysteries?"

Philip looked away, disappointed, and Saul cursed his failure to understand his brother's needs. He never knew the right thing to say. It always felt like the answer was locked inside a riddle that only Philip himself could decode.

"You mean like the clock?"

Philip said nothing; the moment had passed. His attention had been reclaimed by the dismantled timepiece on the desk. He pored over the pieces with the tweezers, delicately rearranging the cogs.

"I saw a mystery earlier," Saul said. "When you were walking across the field. It looked like you disappeared for a while."

Philip paused and turned back to look at Saul. His eyes were fully open now and he was staring at his brother with mild interest.

"Have you heard of CCD, Saul?"

Saul shook his head.

"It stands for Colony Collapse Disorder. It seems that beekeepers in America visited their hives to discover that their bees had disappeared. There was no evidence of predators, no dead bees in sight, and no indication of disease. The bees simply vanished and never returned home."

There was a moment's silence as Philip allowed Saul to process this information.

"You see, Saul, not everything in the natural world can be easily understood. There are always...*irregularities*."

Philip smiled and Saul thought he saw a spark of amusement in his brother's eyes.

"Is it nice?" he said. "The place you disappear to?"

Philip closed his eyes and Saul imagined him conjuring up a vision of his wonderland, delivering himself beyond the limits of his ordinary world.

Philip opened his eyes and gazed at Saul. "I don't remember," he said.

Saul wandered downstairs, his mind still reeling after listening to his brother's disconnected commentary on the flexibility of time. He pictured the clock, in pieces, on Philip's desk and marveled at the level of intensity with which his brother was invested in these crackpot schemes. When Philip talked about reversing time, it was clear that he had really committed himself to unpicking the axiom by which the universe was bound. Saul smiled at the preposterousness of it, but then stopped as a heartbreaking thought occurred to him. Perhaps the reason Philip was trying to turn back time was simply because, in his own clumsy, awkward way, he wanted to be normal again; returned to the boy he was before Cotard's syndrome transformed him into a child besotted with death and decay.

The notion made Saul feel weak, and he struggled to draw breath at the thought that the real Philip might still be in there, fighting his way to get out. He knew the enterprise was impossible, but he wished his brother well all the same; he silently prayed that the complex geometry of the cogs and springs inside the clock released their secret and allowed Philip to travel back to a time before all the strangeness began. That would be a blessing, he thought, not just for Philip, but for the whole family. They were hurting badly and they needed healing. Even Amy could sense it. Saul thought that nothing short of a miracle would drop them meekly into one another's arms, where they could slowly rebuild what they'd lost.

He moved down the hall and passed the open door of the lounge. Father was still planted in the ratty Chesterfield reading the print off yesterday's red top. Saul paused and stood in the doorway, watching Father's eyes scan the page. His pupils were moving at dizzying speed, like ball bearings being shaken in a tin, and for an alarming instant Saul wondered whether Father was having a mild seizure.

"If you're waiting to take my drinks order," he said, his head still buried in the newspaper, "I'll have a cold one from the fridge."

Saul nodded, but stood his ground. Eventually, Father sighed and glanced up.

"What's he done now?" he said. Saul thought he looked utterly defeated, as though his life was nothing more than a succession of failures and anticipated mistakes.

"Nothing," Saul said. "He's taking apart an old clock, trying to see how it works."

Father grunted. "Sounds almost normal. Keep an eye on him, Saul. I dare say there's more to it than that."

Saul considered the bradawl in Philip's steady hand, the quest to reverse time, and said nothing. If Father got even a whiff of what was going on in Philip's room, the jig would be up. Not because Philip couldn't be trusted with simple tools, but because Father was terrified of his own son challenging the natural order of things, where people went to work and read newspapers and drank beer; where the day passed in a blur of hollow routine.

"Anything else?" Father added, noticing that Saul hadn't moved.

Saul paused for a moment, thinking, and then said: "Maybe he just likes mysteries."

Father frowned, failing to understand the reference or the sentiment behind it. Saul nodded, expecting nothing less, and walked on into the kitchen. He fetched his father a drink.

The house was quiet. Saul had checked on Philip, who remained immersed in his pursuit of the impossible; Father was drinking his first beer of the day and still poring over yesterday's news.

Saul drifted outside and glanced up at the sky. It looked wider than he remembered, a vast expanse of unspoilt beauty. It was blue and cloudless, and reminded him of Philip's steady, unblinking eye. He looked away, feeling oddly unsettled, and walked into the adjacent yard towards Bernard Putts' workshop. He wasn't sure why he was revisiting the old carpenter. He had just enjoyed listening to him talk. That seemed as valid a reason as any, and Saul didn't seek to question it. He sauntered towards the workshop and peered through the half-open door.

"Morning, Mr. Putts."

Bernard glanced up from varnishing a decorative umbrella stand. He had a surprised look on his face; in his hand he held a large paint brush.

"Ah! Young Saul. Come to bring me that mug of tea you forgot last time, have you?"

Saul looked horrified, as though he'd committed a mortal sin and then deliberately failed to confess it.

Bernard laughed. "It's okay," he said. "I'm just pulling your leg, son. You'll have to indulge an old man his mischief now and then. Keeps the men in white coats away."

Saul looked a little lost and Bernard laughed again. It was hard not to; the boy's face was a picture of confusion and self-reproach.

"How's your brother?" Bernard said, moving the conversation onto firmer ground. He continued varnishing the umbrella stand and Saul took another tentative step inside the workshop.

"He's trying to unlock the secret of time," he said.

Bernard chuckled. "He might just do it, too, knowing Philip. He has the curiosity of a cat, that one."

Saul looked surprised. "You think it's possible?" he said.

Bernard stopped varnishing and stared at Saul; his eyes were bright and a quick smile appeared, barely noticeable.

"Don't you?" he said.

Saul thought about it for a moment. "You don't think he's crazy?"

"Why would I think that?" Bernard said. "Your brother's a dreamer, Saul, and dreamers have the capacity to change the world."

Saul's brow furrowed in disbelief. "Even Philip?"

"Especially Philip. His eyes see things that others don't. That's what makes him so remarkable."

Saul listened to what Bernard was saying and felt a stab of

resentment. He wasn't sure why, but it seemed unnatural to him that someone might characterize Philip in this way. Saul was used to hearing Father rail against his brother's insanity. Now, to hear Bernard talk of him as though Philip were somehow special, left Saul feeling momentarily jealous.

"I never thought of it that way," he said.

Bernard moved the brush seamlessly across the wood. "I doubt many people do," he said.

"I saw him disappear," Saul said. The words surprised him; it had been something he intended to keep to himself. Bernard stopped varnishing and glanced up. His creased face looked as gnarled and brown as the wood.

"When was this?"

Bernard's sudden interest made Saul feel uncomfortable. He was already regretting opening his mouth.

He shrugged. "It was misty," he said, trying to smile. "It looked like he was flickering, like a faulty hologram or something. It must have been an optical illusion."

Bernard stared at Saul and nodded. "The light can play funny tricks on the mind," he said, and then returned to his varnishing. Saul waited a moment, but Bernard said nothing more. He looked deep in thought, and it occurred to Saul that in his time the old carpenter might have seen a miracle or two of his own.

"Philip can be kind of weird sometimes. It's like he's from a different universe. Father says he arrived late at night in a pod."

Bernard smiled. "Makes about as much sense as anything else," he said.

"I miss him," Saul said simply. "He used to be like a normal brother. Now he's someone I barely even know."

Bernard put down his brush and seated himself on a weathered stool.

"He's still there," he said. "You just have to look a little harder.

He's like a crab, your brother. Sometimes he buries himself under the rocks."

Saul considered this for a moment and shivered. He had nightmares enough already; the idea of Philip as a scuttling crab-monster, dragging itself towards him on swollen claws, was not one he was keen to entertain.

"Father says that one day he'll tip himself so far over the edge he won't be able to get back."

"That's just because he's afraid, Saul. You feel like you've lost a brother, but your parents feel like they're losing a son. They see him drifting further and further away from them with each passing day. They have every right to feel terrified."

"Amy sometimes watches him for hours, like he's a strange creature from another planet."

Bernard smiled again. "She's starting over," he said. "You all are. You're rediscovering who he is, that's all. Learning his behavior and routines, just like you would a newborn baby."

Saul listened attentively and realized that Bernard's simple outward appearance masked a much more sophisticated under-standing of his family's situation. Compared to his father, Bernard possessed an awareness of Philip's fragile mental state that Saul found oddly comforting. It was like listening to a doctor, he thought, or a therapist—someone who knew more than he was letting on.

Bernard nodded his head, as though silently acknowledging the end of the conversation, picked up his paint brush and dipped it into the tin of varnish. With hypnotic, easy strokes, he patiently applied another layer of gloss to the umbrella stand.

Saul watched him for a moment and then took another long look around Bernard's cluttered workshop. If anything, it appeared even more disorganized than his previous visit, as though the furniture and the wooden sculptures had cloned themselves in the time between. He suddenly remembered his brother's drawing, the one of a shaded, empty landscape that Philip had called the Fade. He maneuvered himself through the confusion of off-cut timber and neglected tools, and drew alongside the worktop where he'd first caught sight of it. He rummaged among the chaos of blueprints and sketches that qualified as Bernard's office and found the A3 sheet of paper, slightly crumpled now, lying beneath a steel skewer that pierced the heart of several dozen mimeographed receipts.

Saul eased the drawing from its burial place and held it up to the light. There was the small boy, looking lost and alone, in the middle of a vast, unearthly dimension, where the grey horizon stretched endlessly across the myriad shades of the page towards the shore. As Saul looked upon it, it filled him with a fleeting current of dread, as though an electrical charge had been passed through the entire length of his body.

"This picture," he said. "Can I take it back to Philip?"

Bernard glanced up, barely even aware that the boy was still there, and gestured for him to take it. Saul rolled it up and stuck the drawing under his arm.

"Bye, Mr. Putts," he said. "I'll tell Philip you said hi."

Bernard offered a perfunctory wave and returned to his work. Saul left the workshop and ran across the yard. His heart was racing, but he couldn't fully appreciate why. He hurtled into the house and slammed the back door. He felt suddenly tense. With the drawing clamped against his side, he went off in search of Philip, determined to discover more about the Fade.

Within minutes of re-entering the house, Saul heard a commotion upstairs. Father's voice was raised and Saul could detect a frayed quality to it as it climbed steadily from frustration to rage. He seemed to be shouting to an empty room as Saul could hear no retort from an opponent, but he visualized Philip sitting at his desk, pretending he couldn't hear, his expression unreadable, his disinterest in the situation inevitably making the whole thing worse.

Saul braced himself and ran up the stairs, not even bothering to try and second-guess what he might find. It was just as well. He rounded the newel post at the top of the stairs and gazed into the open door of Philip's bedroom. Father stood in the middle of the room, red-faced, arms folded and ready to explode. He turned when he heard Saul reach the landing.

"Look at him!" Father said. "It's way past a joke, Saul. It stopped being funny a long time ago. This is just bloody ludicrous!" He threw his hands into the air and took a step back. He looked wrung-out and Saul remembered he'd just taken on his first beer of the day when he'd left to see Mr. Putts. Perhaps he thought he was dreaming; perhaps he hoped this entire scene was being played out in his head like a fragmented nightmare, quickly spilling over into farce.

He stared past Father and watched Philip who, as he'd suspected, was silently sitting at his desk. In front of him was a large tub of butter. As Saul looked on, he dipped his hands into the container and pulled them out laden with gloopy deposits of fat, which he promptly applied to his face and rubbed into his skin.

"Apparently butter is the perfect embalming agent," Father said incredulously. "Can you believe it, Saul? *Embalming!*"

"He said that?"

Father looked back at him and he saw a man weighed down with conflicting emotions. Fury certainly, but also a spiraling wretchedness, which was eating away at him like an infection.

"Dead people need to be embalmed, he said. The butter will fill the pores with fat and prevent decay. He said an Indian healer showed him how to do it in a dream."

Father still sounded agitated beyond measure, but there was an underlying lassitude too, born of bone-weary familiarity with Philip's unstable pathology. He looked like a man staring his own personal failure full in the face. It made Saul want to drag him out of the room and scream Mr. Putts' advice at him: *You just have to look a little harder. He's like a crab...Sometimes he buries himself under the rocks.*

Saul looked at his brother and felt a wave of pity engulf him. His cheeks and brow were slick with grease, and he reminded Saul of a Christmas turkey basted with dripping fat.

"Philip," he said. His brother turned towards him, face slack and impassive. "I think that's enough now. If you put too much on it might not work as well. Didn't the healer tell you to be careful?"

Father stared at Saul as though he'd lost his mind. The idea that Saul might somehow be colluding in Philip's lunacy was a madness too far. He'd already lost one son to this foolishness; he wasn't prepared to concede another without a fight.

"What the hell is wrong with you?" he hissed. "If you play along with this shit, he'll never understand how crazy it is! He'll just keep doing it until we all end up in a rubber room!"

Saul held up a hand, warding off his father's disapproval. He didn't even look at him; he focused instead solely on Philip.

"Time to stop?" he said.

Philip stared at his buttery hands, glanced at Saul, smiled briefly and nodded. He put the lid back on the tub of butter and rose from the chair. He walked past Father without uttering a word, passed by Saul, who was hovering on the threshold of the room, and slowly descended the stairs.

Father held a hand to his brow and exhaled heavily. Weak sunlight shone through the window and fell across his face. Saul could see the deep creases etched across the slope of his brow.

"I don't even know who he is anymore," Father whispered, as

much to himself as to Saul. There wasn't much Saul felt equipped to say by way of reply. Instead, he turned and followed Philip down the stairs, leaving Father alone in the butter-scented room.

—————

As Saul reached the bottom of the stairs he saw Philip leave the house via the back door. He considered giving chase, but decided that, given the circumstances, now was not the time to pursue him to ask about the Fade. That particular dialogue would have to wait, preferably for an occasion when his brother's cheeks were not weeping butter and Father's howling lament no longer echoed around the house.

He walked towards the kitchen and realized he was still holding Philip's drawing under his arm. He removed it and placed it on the kitchen table, where it started to unroll. The sweeping grey landscape unfurled a little and he caught a fleeting glimpse of the boy overlooking the great mystery of the place, assimilating the vast plains, bereft of life, complicated only by its infinite expanse.

Saul shook his head, lost for a moment in the strangeness of the drawing, as a voice behind him said: "What's that?"

It was Amy, returning from her friend's house, as alert as ever to the slightest tremor in Saul's demeanor.

"Nothing," he said, reaching for the rolled-up paper. "Just a drawing."

"Can I see it?"

Saul shook his head. "It belongs to Philip. If you want to see it you'll have to ask him."

Amy stood in the centre of the kitchen. Her face was pale and unblemished, like an unglazed mask. She stared at Saul with knowing eyes, far beyond her years. He thought again of the boy in the drawing, standing in the middle of an unknown vista, staring at nothing. He looked again at Amy and marveled at her resilience. He tried to imagine what it must be like growing up in such a profoundly disturbing world.

"What did he draw?" she asked.

Saul smiled at her cunning. "That would be almost the same as seeing it," he said. "Besides, I don't really know what it is. It's like looking directly into Philip's head, at the stuff locked away inside. You sure you want to see such a thing?"

Amy solemnly nodded her head, as though she had been asked to keep a State secret.

"How much crazier can it be than all the other stuff he does?" she said.

Saul laughed and wedged the drawing under his arm. "Why be in such a hurry to find out?"

Saul went upstairs and hid the drawing under his bed. When he came back down, Father was watching TV in the front room. He could hear Amy pottering around in the kitchen, probably peeling the potatoes so that Mother didn't have to when she returned from her trip to the shops. Saul swallowed hard, feeling such a wave of love for his sister it was difficult to breathe. He wanted to go back into the kitchen and hug her till she screamed, but he knew he never would. The poor kid would be terrified. Amy often made him feel like this and he couldn't determine whether it was love that he felt or pity, or an odd combination of the two. Either way, he knew she was the family's centre, rich in spirit and stronger than the rest of them combined.

He moved into the front room and Father looked at him from his armchair, his eyes red and clouded over with whatever memory had been haunting his television dream.

"Where's your mother?" he said.

Saul shrugged and seated himself on the tired-looking sofa. "Still shopping."

Father rubbed his eyes. Saul watched him closely; the man seemed to sink into himself whenever he found the weight of reality too much to bear. He stared at his hands as though failing to understand what they were for.

Saul noticed him glance at the clock above the fireplace.

"She's been gone a long time," Father said.

Saul nodded, not knowing what else to say.

"What about your brother?" He looked tense when he spoke of Philip, a feeling that derived from never knowing what to expect next.

"He's out, too," Saul said. "Wandering in the fields some-where, I imagine." He received another jolt as the image of the boy in the grey space of the Fade came rushing back at him, forcing Saul into a realization: the lost boy in the Fade was *Philip*. Only, he wasn't lost at all; quite the opposite. The boy in the drawing had discovered a place where he felt perfectly at home; he had found peace, in the unchanging silence of the Fade.

Father adjusted himself in the armchair and reached for the TV remote. He pointed it at the screen in front of him, surfed the flickering reality shows, and then turned to Saul.

"Why do you think he does those things?" he said softly.

Saul drew in a breath, surprised by the question, and a heavy silence settled in the room.

"You know why," he said eventually. "We all do. The doctors explained it to us."

Father pulled a face, as he always did when doctors were mentioned.

"What do they know? It's all trial and error, Saul. That's how they work. Eliminating one illness at a time. It's bollocks and you know it."

He certainly knew Father's opinion of the medical profession;

he'd heard this tainted rhetoric many times before. The health system was like a broken machine, spitting out patients in an arbitrary fashion; some healed, some not. He decided it was best not to get Father started on one of his rants.

"It doesn't matter anyway," he said. "It's all taken care of. It was only butter. We should be grateful it wasn't something more serious."

Father stared at him, appalled. "What *could* it have been, Saul? Motor oil? Blood? The smeared intestines of a young child?"

Saul grimaced and looked away. "That's just daft," he said. "Philip would never do something like that."

There was a lengthy pause before Father said: "How can you be so sure?"

Saul stared at the elaborate patterns in the carpet. The truth was, he couldn't be certain of anything, not where Philip was concerned. He closed his eyes for a moment and the image of his brother's face dripping with viscera and blood came all too easily to mind. Who knew what Philip might dream up next? Not the doctors, that was increasingly apparent, nor anyone in the family. Only the person in Philip's head knew; that strange little boy who stood in the middle of nowhere, staring out at a distant shore.

When Philip returned later on that evening Saul was waiting for him in his bedroom. He had pinned the drawing of the Fade to the wall above the bed. If it had been in a frame, one might easily have imagined it belonged there.

Philip noticed the drawing almost immediately and smiled.

"You found it," he said.

Saul frowned. "Was I supposed to?"

Philip shrugged. He had been collecting stones on his travels and he was busy emptying his pockets. He lined them up on the window sill and began counting them.

"Fifteen," he said. He glanced at Saul proudly. "I found fifteen."

"I'm more interested in the picture," Saul said. "Did you draw it, Philip?"

His brother stared at the image on the wall and smiled again. Looking at it seemed to relax him; that was always a good sign with Philip. So many things these days seemed to frustrate him.

"It's the Fade," he said. "That's where I live."

Saul froze, trying to work through the complex logic of Philip's thought processes. Much of what he said could be ignored; but every now and then, randomly scattered among the nonsense, would be elements of truth. The skill was learning to filter one from the other.

"What do you mean it's where you live?" Saul said, playing along with Philip's game, as he so often did these days. But Philip wasn't interested in following the path of Saul's dialogue; he was determined to create a path of his own.

"That boy," he said, staring intently at the figure in the drawing. "Look how happy he is."

The observation took Saul by surprise. It was impossible to gauge the mood of the boy because he had his back to the viewer, but hadn't he made a judgment of his own on first viewing? Hadn't he assumed the boy in the drawing to be lost? Had he not thought of the boy as lonely and without hope?

Saul looked closely at the drawing again, trying to detect what Philip saw in the image, but failing. All he could see was an isolated child stranded in a forsaken land.

"Why is he happy?" Saul said.

Philip turned and watched him for a moment, as though Saul was being deliberately obtuse. When he was satisfied that his brother had asked the question in good faith, Philip said: "Because he's safe."

Saul stared at the picture again and realized it was as good an answer as any he was likely to get. The boy *was* safe. He was alone in the Fade, but nothing from this world or the next could harm him while he stood in the grey shadows overlooking the hills.

Saul turned back to his brother and held his gaze for a moment. "Are you the boy in the picture, Philip?" he said.

Philip laughed and began recounting the stones.

"No," he said. "That's a different boy. I haven't found him yet."

Saul reached out and squeezed his brother's arm. "Who is it?" he said, suddenly eager to know.

But Philip had pulled away and lost interest. The stones were infinitely more captivating. As Saul looked on, Philip began polishing their surfaces with his sleeve, the boy in the drawing no more than a distant flicker along a misfiring synapse of the brain.

6

OPEN GROUND

The ice cream van drew into the barn and ground to a halt. Bunce applied the handbrake and rose from his seat behind the wheel. His apron was still covered in the red and white gunk of the crushed ice cream and he removed it and folded it into a ball. He placed it on the black vinyl of the driver's seat and tried to control his breathing. His heart was racing. He knew implicitly that his world had changed forever; that what he had done that afternoon in the quiet suburban lane would change everything. He had been caught beneath the wheels of an onrushing train and the young man he had imagined himself to be was now split into something else entirely, something he barely even recognized. The Hilary Bunce that had woken up that morning, riddled with doubt and insecurity, was gone. In its place was a creature who had abducted a young boy; a creature who feared nothing; a creature who felt blood thundering in the swollen flux of its veins.

Bunce turned around and stared at the bound figure lying on the floor of the van. The boy was still unconscious. His face was flat and without expression. Bunce was startled by how young he looked. The venom that had coursed through the boy's body earlier in the day had twisted his features into something monstrous. Now he just looked like a kid, lost in the frenzy of whatever dream-life he was conjuring in his sleep.

Bunce stared at him for a moment, mesmerized by the silver pin driven through the kid's eyebrow. He wondered if the boy's mother was already starting to worry, already fearing the worst. He thought about his own Ma and felt a profound sense of loss. God, he missed her so much. If she'd still been around everything would have been so different. A sudden thought, black and insidious, filled his head and he closed his eyes to try and dislodge it. It made no difference. All he could see in his mind's eye was the severed finger bearing Ma's wedding band buried in the box underground. He shook his head and the image changed, as though he were turning the wheel of a kaleidoscope. In its place the disdainful face of Fliss appeared, eyes hard and watchful, assessing Bunce's new condition and still finding it wanting.

The boy began to stir and Bunce knelt down beside him to shove the rag back into his mouth. He hesitated and when the boy's eyes flickered open Bunce watched the horror of the situation settle across his features like a storm cloud occluding the sun. The boy opened his mouth to scream and Bunce quickly thrust the rag between his lips.

"No need for that," he said. "It's pointless anyway. There's no one around to hear."

The boy's eyes were wide and unblinking, frozen in fear, his terror deepening by the second. Bunce thought he looked like a trussed rabbit waiting to be skinned and he giggled a little, despite himself. He placed a hand over his mouth and looked into the boy's eyes.

"If I remove the rag I want you to promise you won't scream. Okay?"

The boy nodded. Bunce slowly removed the gag and waited.

The boy watched him for a moment and then screamed bloody murder, thrashing his head wildly from side to side. Bunce smacked him hard around the face with the back of his hand and the boy stopped instantly. He looked visibly shaken; his face bore a large red mark across the right cheek. Bunce noticed that the boy was staring at him like an animal might stare at a predator, braced for the inevitable killer blow. The boy's assessment of Bunce, like much else today, had changed. No longer did he regard him with cold, implacable eyes; now he saw Bunce for what he really was: a man whose moral compass had come loose.

"Do I need to put this in your mouth?" Bunce said, holding up the rag.

The boy looked at him for a moment, trying to think his way through the question, and then shook his head.

"Good. What's your name?"

The boy remained silent.

"Do you want to know mine?" Bunce said.

The boy's eyes widened and he shook his head. Bunce smiled; he was a smart kid. He clearly realized that the more he knew of Bunce the less chance he had of walking out of this thing alive.

"David," he said softly. "My name's David."

"Hmmm. How interesting. I had you pegged as a Ricky or a Vinny. You know, because of the pin."

The boy looked confused and Bunce pressed on. "Tell me, David, why do you think you're here today? Do you have any idea?"

David thought for a moment and then said: "Because you're crazy."

Bunce smiled again, pleased to discover that the boy still had a little fire in his belly. No doubt he would find it useful in the Fade.

"No," he said, "that isn't it, David. It's something far less melodramatic. You're here because you made a mistake. You treated me like a dog, just like everyone else. Have you ever looked into a dog's mouth, David, and seen how sharp their teeth are? Have you ever thought what it might be like if one day that same dog decided to turn? Those teeth could rip your face off, David. Those teeth could quite easily tear you apart."

The boy studied him, his eyes darting around the van's interior, looking for a possible means of escape. Bunce found it amusing how predictable all this was. Human nature seemed to dictate that, even in captivity, the only thing left to cling to was hope. It was an exercise in futility, and both he and the boy knew it. David belonged to him now, to do with as he pleased. Their place in the world had been altered in that crude thirty second exchange in the suburban lane. The shapes they assumed in the darkness would be forever changed.

"You should always be mindful of dogs," Bunce said, turning the boy over and tightening the twine that bound his hands and feet. "You never know what's going on inside their silly heads." He glanced up at David and grinned. "So. Shall we get started?"

Bunce lodged the rag deep into David's mouth and lifted him with terrifying ease over his left shoulder, as though he were carrying a sack of grain. He exited the van and carried the boy deep into the barn. He could smell chicken shit and the seeping freshness of baled hay. It was cool and dark; arrows of light pierced the wooden structure and guided him towards the barn's mezzanine. He carried the boy up the ladder, adjusting the meager weight as he climbed, and shuffled through the blanket of straw that lay in his path. In the far corner of the mezzanine, where the gathered straw was thickest, Bunce set the boy down and removed the rag.

"Same deal applies here as before," he said. "Any screaming and you'll most likely cop for it. Understood?"

David nodded. Bunce observed him as he looked around the barn, that same wild hope in his eyes. It was almost heartbreaking to watch; the boy still had no real sense of how desperate things had become.

"Don't get too comfortable. This place is only temporary. I've booked you into a very special place indeed. I think you'll like it there, David, I really do. And you'll have plenty of time to consider what you've done."

David stared at him with a hint of that familiar defiance; his eyebrows furrowed and the silver pin buried there flashed like a shooting star.

"I haven't done anything," he said. "*You* have." The stare grew harder and Bunce felt a sudden tightness in his chest. "Aren't you afraid of what they'll do to you when they eventually find you? Aren't you fucking terrified?"

Bunce shook his head, confused. He felt flustered again, unsure of himself. What was the stupid boy doing? *He* was the one who was supposed to be terrified; it was *his* world that had been shaken upside down, *his* universe that had imploded. Bunce ran a hand across his balding skull, trying to figure out what had gone wrong. Perhaps he hadn't made his point firmly enough; maybe he hadn't made himself at all clear to the poor boy. He felt a flicker of unease as he remembered the fat, humiliated entity he used to be. Had the boy not fully recognized that Bunce was a changed man? Did he not see that he was no longer a victim but a master of his own circumstance, who controlled not only his own fate, but the boy's as well?

He felt the blood pounding in his head as the rage began to mount. He had known failure all his life and was sick of it; had known shame and humiliation, too. He looked at the boy and saw only a dull representation of everything he hated in the world, everything that had ground him into the very earth on which he stood. He was more than the bovine simpleton that everyone saw when they cast their eyes upon him, and he aimed to prove it. He was Hilary Bunce. His face turned red and his eyes blazed with anger. He was Hilary Bunce, by God! The world would know his name soon enough.

He lunged forward and knocked the boy into the straw. He bent over him and fed the rag deep into his mouth. David tried to protest and struggle free, but Bunce was easily three times heavier, and the boy was pinned awkwardly beneath his weight. He looked deep into David's eyes and at last saw the kind of terror he had been hoping for. He smiled, gratified that the boy finally understood the dark current underpinning this entire enterprise.

"I am Hilary Bunce," he said softly. "It might pay to remember my name."

He reached forward with his hands, held the boy's head steady, and ripped the silver pin through the flesh above David's eye. The boy screamed into the rag and Bunce watched as his face turned puce and then began to pale as his eyes flickered towards unconsciousness. Blood began to stream down the boy's face and Bunce let it run, marveling at the course it weaved across David's ashen cheek. He held the silver pin in the air where it glinted in an arrow of light.

"Hilary Bunce," he repeated, looking down at the boy in the straw. But David was no longer listening; a black tide had carried him away.

When David came round, he felt an instant throbbing above his right eye as though a tumor had been inexpertly removed. His eyes fluttered open around a crusted rim of dried blood and gazed upon the white moon of Bunce's smiling face. He shuddered and tried to retreat into the yielding straw, but Bunce had a firm hold of his hooded top. David realized, with a mounting sense of unease, that he was going nowhere.

"Welcome back," Bunce said. "You managed to slip the leash there for a few minutes, David. I thought for a horrifying moment that you'd found your own way to the Fade."

David frowned; it felt like he had wandered into Bunce's mad world halfway through a conversation that only his abductor could possibly understand.

"I want to go home," he muttered. "I won't say anything, I promise. I just want everything to go back to how it was."

Bunce's smile widened; he looked like a grinning pig, David thought, with small beady eyes and bright pink skin. The boy had never been more terrified in his life.

"Too late for that, David. That boat has sailed, I'm afraid. What we face now is what my Ma used to call the point of no return. We're committed, you see, both of us. There's no going back. Not now; probably not ever. All we have left is the Fade."

There was a long moment of silence, during which David stared into the bright eyes of Hilary Bunce. Eventually he said: "Are you going to kill me?"

Bunce threw back his head and laughed. "Why on earth would I want to do that? You just need a new perspective, that's all; a change of scenery. It'll do you the world of good, I'm sure."

David looked more confused than ever and Bunce held his breath, already beginning to draw himself into the ethereal mists of the Fade. He leaned over David's body and gently laid his hands on the boy's brittle skull.

"Close your eyes," he whispered. He glanced down and saw that David had followed the instruction without hesitation. His bottom lip was trembling; his head felt like a small melon beneath Bunce's large, uncompromising hands.

"Clear your mind of thought," Bunce said, "otherwise this

could get very messy. I've never done anything like this before. I don't even know if it'll work."

He felt David start to shake and heard him muttering something vaguely familiar under his breath.

"No prayers," Bunce said. "They're of no value here."

David fell silent; when Bunce looked down he saw that the boy had squeezed his eyes shut as tightly as his facial muscles would allow. A tear or two had escaped; they chased each other down the bloodied track of David's cheek. He closed his own eyes and applied pressure to the boy's skull, attempting to force all thought from David's head. His hands pushed down hard, feeling his way towards the Fade.

"Come on," he muttered. "Don't disappoint me, not now."

His breathing grew heavier and he could feel perspiration trickling down his forehead and onto the flickering lids of his eyes. He pictured the cool landscape that awaited them and focused on pulling himself and the boy towards it. It was proving much harder than usual to reach and Bunce could feel his muscles straining as the borders of his kingdom withdrew.

"God damn it!" he cried, sensing for the first time a stiff resistance at the edges of the Fade and feeling a terror not dissimilar to that of the boy's. He labored with increasing intensity to visualize every particular of the place he cherished, pushing himself to greater and greater feats of recall, walking himself through the wide open spaces, piecing it together in his memory, stitch by intricate stitch.

At last Bunce smiled as he began to feel the cold bubble of the Fade starting to coalesce around them. He opened his eyes and looked upon the cruel terrain that occupied so many of his most unfathomable dreams. The scarred earth and the colorless sky were enveloped in a white haze, and the whole place had the air of something stillborn, as though it had been some lost deity's first attempt at creation before being judiciously aborted. The Fade looked cold and unpopulated, as it always had. A region that had accepted only a handful of footprints; a state that existed solely at the frayed edges of mankind's conflicted imagination.

Bunce stared out at the strange prism of light that stretched before him, dazzled by its intelligent design. Beyond the haze of light that flowed outward from the centre of its own darkness, he could still see the limiting dimensions of the barn. There was the straw, the baled hay, the rusty tools that Pa had long ago discarded. Everything was still there, flickering beyond the concentrated measure of the Fade, existing almost outside itself, as a place he only vaguely remembered, like a nightmare flushed from the mind.

Bunce smiled and removed his hands from David's head.

"You can open your eyes now," he said.

He watched the boy carefully, uncertain whether the Fade would declare itself to another, his knowledge limited, the laws that might allow such a thing far beyond his ability to comprehend.

"Do you see it?" Bunce asked; but the question was unnecessary. He could tell by the sharp intake of breath and the wide eyes that David was experiencing his first glimpse of Bunce's hallowed land.

"You drugged me," the boy said. He turned to Bunce, seeking some kind of logical explanation for the mystery that lay before him. "I'm hallucinating, aren't I? I must be; I can see the sky and the hills...and the sea."

Bunce smiled and shook his head. "No hallucination, David. This is the Fade. It's where I come when I need to be alone."

David turned back and took in the vast sprawl of the empty land that led towards the distant shore. Bunce could almost hear the boy's accelerated heartbeat hammering inside his chest.

"I want to go home," David said, unable to avert his eyes from the impossible vista. "Please. Just take me home."

Bunce touched him lightly on the shoulder, feeling the weight of a complex sorrow he knew he would never be able to allay.

"You are home," he said softly, looking out across the Fade. "This is where I think you belong."

When Bunce returned to the farm house he felt a calmness radiating from somewhere deep inside. That the boy would stay trapped in the Fade until he decided otherwise had left him feeling strangely relaxed, at peace with both his resolution of the matter and the moral imperative that had driven it in the first place. David was perfectly safe; the Fade would hold him like an insect in amber, buried beneath countless layers of silt and clay. It made Bunce smile just thinking about it. The boy was in the one place where no one would find him. He might as well have been lifted from the face of the earth. The notion gave Bunce a powerful sense of comfort and relief and he smiled again, pleased with his afternoon's work. Today, he wasn't a man, he was a god, and before all of this was over David would learn to kneel at his feet and shower him with kisses, just like a good disciple should.

Bunce entered the kitchen and raided the fridge while there was no one around to berate him. He drank half a bottle of milk, wiped the glass rim with the back of his hand, and returned it to its place on the shelf. He followed this by breaking off a slab of Stilton with his large, unwashed hands and nibbling at it like a mouse as he walked.

He began climbing the stairs, but stopped halfway up when he heard movement in one of the rooms. Gilly must be home, he thought, sleeping off one of his mindless military exercises that seemed to occupy so many of his afternoons. Bunce had always been unable to fathom quite why he spent so much time training; what he was preparing for was anybody's guess. There was a war raging inside Gilly's head, of that he had no doubt. God help them all if ever it spilled out beyond the psychosis in which his brother was trapped.

Bunce climbed another few steps up the stairs and saw Gilly's door slowly begin to open. Before he could utter a word, Fliss floated across the landing bearing the hint of a smile. She turned and noticed Bunce on the stairs and her smile vanished, as though it had only ever been a fleeting illusion.

"Jesus," she said. "What the hell are you doing creeping up on people like that? You gave me quite a fright."

Bunce could see that; her face was flushed and her eyes were darting between the stairs and Gilly's room. She looked like she'd just remembered she'd left the oven on.

"You aren't allowed in there," he said. "If Gilly knew you'd been in his room, he'd go berserk."

Fliss looked momentarily flustered. "Yes, well, he asked me to, didn't he? Wanted me to give his dungeon a Spring clean. Or do I have to seek your approval first?"

Bunce ignored this last comment and glanced down at her hands. They were empty. He breathed in through his nose, trying to detect the aroma of cleaning products in the air. All he could smell was the lingering dankness of the house.

"You don't have any equipment," he said. "Doesn't that make it a little hard to clean?"

Her eyes narrowed and she stared at him with mild curiosity, puzzled by his sudden boldness.

"I haven't finished," she said. "I still have another unit to sort out. Not that it's any of your damn business."

He stared at her for a moment and almost called her bluff. He wanted to brush past her and step into Gilly's room, but a large part of him was afraid of what fresh horror he might discover inside. He thought he could still hear movement on the other side of the door. If he probed too hard he suspected he might be the one who ended up regretting it. He could hear the rhythm of some awful betrayal pulsing inside his head. He surrendered to it for a while and then tried to block it out, but it was insidious, like a toxic gas being slowly released, a devastating message sent on an ill wind to pierce his tender heart.

He thought for a moment of David, alone in the Fade, battling his terror of the unknown, before he turned on his heels and walked slowly back down the stairs. He sensed Fliss watching him go, could hear her labored breathing, as though the exchange had caught her off-guard, pushing her to the very edge of naming the awful deception that lay behind Gilly's bedroom door.

He needed fresh air. His head felt woolly and hot and he could feel his cheeks burning. He pressed the palms of his hands against his skull and pushed into the unyielding bone. There was too much stuff crammed inside his brain, too much clutter wedged in there, just waiting to bring him to his knees.

He stumbled through the kitchen and dragged himself into the cobbled yard, where he propped himself against the wall of the house and drew in a huge lungful of cooling air. It made him feel light-headed for a moment, and when he looked up he thought he saw Ma walking towards him across the open field beyond the house. He closed his eyes and tried to compose himself. When he opened them again, he realized it wasn't Ma walking towards him, it was Pa: head bowed, boots heavy with woodland mud, trailing a shovel in his right hand, which was bouncing across the furrowed earth.

Bunce watched him close the distance between them until

eventually Pa drew level with the yard. It was only at this point that he glanced up. He looked surprised to see his son angled against the wall of the farmhouse, still breathing hard. There was an expression on his face that Bunce struggled to read, as though the journey across the field into the woods had complicated Pa's existence. He looked like a man driven by unnatural impulse, the muscles in his arms tense, the wildness in his eyes undimmed. He lifted the shovel so that it didn't scream as it was dragged along the cobbles and stared thoughtfully at his son, waiting for him to speak.

"Been digging?" Bunce said, trying to ease Pa into a conversation he looked disinclined to endure.

Pa hesitated and then pointed in the direction of the woods. "I planted a sapling in one of the clearings. For your Ma. Thought she might like it."

Bunce nodded, wondering if he'd planted it on top of the wooden box bearing Ma's severed finger. Perhaps Pa thought that by planting the tree he could somehow alleviate his guilt. Was he hoping that the sowing of new life might compensate for whatever outrage had befallen Ma? Bunce looked away. He felt physically sick. He glanced down at Pa's hands and noticed that he was still wearing a pair of green heavy-duty gardening gloves. His fingers looked huge, like those of a clown; each one had been anointed with a dark coating of mud.

"That sounds nice," Bunce said. "The tree of life, right?"

Pa smiled and moved across the yard towards the outhouse. Bunce followed, keeping a discreet distance, not quite ready to pass up the opportunity to have his father's company to himself for a change. He watched Pa clean the blade of the shovel, open the outhouse door, and hang the tool back on its rightful peg on the wall. When he turned round he seemed mildly curious as to why Bunce might still be there.

"Is there anything else, Hilary?"

Bunce paused, not certain how to begin, and then simply said: "Fliss was mean again, Pa. I don't think she likes me one bit."

Pa sighed and closed the outhouse door. "You two have to learn to get along. It ain't easy without your mother, Hilary, you know that. We need all the help we can get."

Bunce pounced, as if he'd been waiting for just this occasion to articulate a radical idea. "We could get a cleaner," he said. "Or a live-in maid. Anything would be better than Fliss, Pa. She's not family, and never will be. She'll never be able to replace Ma."

Pa's gloved hand shot out with the force of a piston and struck Bunce across the side of the face.

"*Hold your goddamn tongue!*" he said.

Bunce fell to his knees and raised a hand to his face, cowering before his father's rage.

"I hate her, Pa," he said softly. "I hate what she's done to the family. What she's done to you..."

Pa was wheezing like an old man. His face was perspiring and his cheeks were glowing a deep crimson; his eyes were bright with shame. He reached down one of his gloved hands to help his son to his feet, but Bunce withdrew, expecting another assault. His cheek was inflamed and streaked with mud. He was watching Pa through narrow, intimidated eyes.

Pa turned away and held his clown's hands to his face. He pushed his back against the door of the outhouse and slid down until his bottom was resting on the cold cobbles of the yard. Bunce noticed that his whole body was shaking. He wanted to reach out and touch his shoulder, but he wasn't sure if Pa was angry or sad. There was a deep, uncomfortable silence. They both sat on the hard stones, overwhelmed by exhaustion and a lingering confusion.

"Jesus," Pa said. "What the hell's happened to us? How in God's name did we end up like this?"

Bunce had no answer to such a complex question; at least, not one that Pa would want to hear. He stared out across the field to the woodland beyond and thought of Ma and the newly-planted sapling and the severed finger still bearing the ring. It was all too obvious what had happened, Bunce thought: Fliss. *Fliss* had happened. She was the source of all their problems, only Pa couldn't see it. He refused to see what was right in front of his nose.

"She's changed us, Pa," Bunce said, no longer mindful of the consequences. "Each one of us is different. Have you noticed that? It's not like before, when Ma was here, and it never will be again."

Pa smacked the clown hand against his own leg, startling Bunce and sending slivers of mud arcing into the air.

"Stop talking about your damn Ma," he said "It'll do none of us any good. She's gone, lad. We all have to move on."

There was a long pause before Bunce said: "But I miss her, Pa."

He heard Pa emit a long sigh and sensed every ounce of frustration leaving his father's body. What remained was a scooped-out husk, the shell of a man whose purpose was slowly slipping away.

"I do, too, lad. We all do."

They sat in silence for a short time, listening to the rhythmic cadence of the natural world as it sought to impose itself on another fading day. Birds were squabbling in the nearby trees; a low wind swung in from the east and capered in the long grass beneath the hills.

"I don't trust her, you know," Bunce said. "I never have."

Pa turned to look at him, finally removing the gloves. "You mean Ma?"

"No. Fliss. She's not a good person, Pa. I know she's not. In fact, there's something you ought to know. Something I saw."

Bunce sensed a slight change in the atmosphere: a cooling, a distinct lowering of the temperature between them.

"Spit it out then, lad."

Bunce turned to look at his father, feeling suddenly nervous. "I saw her today coming out of Gilly's bedroom. She was smiling."

Pa seemed to freeze and Bunce wondered if he'd just had one of his own suspicions confirmed.

"What the hell are you trying to say?"

Bunce shrugged. "I don't know, Pa, not really. I just..." He paused, composed himself for a moment, then added: "I think there was someone with her in the room."

Pa stared into the distance, focusing on the sky, the distant fields, the hills. At that moment he looked like a man in pain, burdened by the memory of love, with a history of mistakes to confess.

7

FISH

Saul sat at the kitchen table and looked around at his family. They were all eating silently except for Philip, who had failed to take a single bite of the food Mother had painstakingly prepared for them. While Mother, Father and Amy were all tucking into their baked sea bass, Philip was staring intently at his plate. He seemed to be looking closely at the fish, and Saul looked down at his own half-eaten meal with mild curiosity, expecting to see some abnormality revealed in the reconfigured fare before him. When he glanced up again Philip was prodding at his own portion of white meat, as though checking to make sure it was dead.

Saul looked across at Father, who was thankfully too absorbed in his own meal to notice Philip's strange fascination with the fish. Saul knew it was only a matter of time, though, before the delicate balance was lost. If Father happened to look up and catch Philip trying to prod life back into the bloody sea bass, all hell would break loose.

Saul reached under the table and tapped his brother's ankles.

When Philip glanced up, Saul stared at him hard across the table and mouthed: *What the hell are you doing? Eat your damn fish!*

Philip watched him for a moment, an alien assessing an unfamiliar species, and then returned to his obsession with the contents of his plate. Almost inevitably, Philip's growing agitation eventually drew Father's attention, and within seconds of him noticing what was going on a distinct tension developed between them. Saul watched Mother's eyes widen and the slender muscles in her arms grew taut. She was gripping her knife and fork as though her very life depended on her never again letting go.

"Your mother's food not good enough for you, son?" Father said.

Philip didn't even look up; he continued to push his fish around the plate, exploring the hidden geography of a world that none of the others had the imagination or the courage to perceive.

"*Philip!*" Father said, more harshly this time, making Mother and Amy jump a little in their chairs. "Pay attention. I'm talking to you."

Philip did look up this time, mildly surprised by the intrusion, clearly confused to find himself the subject of his father's interest. His empty fork was raised in his left hand and he looked disoriented, as though he'd just been dragged back from the brink of a nightmare.

"What's the matter with your fish?" Father said. His face was turning an unpleasant shade of red, but despite this Saul could see he was trying desperately hard to remain calm.

"Let him be, Frank. It's not important," Mother said. As usual, she was attempting to prevent another head-on collision between husband and son. Mother's life was one that Saul had never been able to understand, and he listened to her now with a deepening sense of child-like sorrow that almost brought tears to his eyes.

"The boy needs to eat, Cynth. Look at him. He's wasting

away." Father raised his glass of beer and Saul watched half of it disappear in one appalling movement of the throat. He turned his attention back to Philip and said, "Stop playing with the bloody thing! Cut it up and eat it, like a normal person. Is that too much to ask?"

"It used to swim," Philip said. "Like this." He pushed his head forward and began opening and closing his mouth; at the same time he moved his arms through the air like fins.

Amy started to laugh and began copying him. Saul watched them both for a moment and then decided to join in, gulping in oxygen like a fish and darting through an invisible sea of air. After a moment Mother chuckled and watched her children delight in this impromptu simulation, marveling at how suddenly bright and alive they looked.

Father slammed his hand on the table, startling everyone and rendering the plates and glasses momentarily airborne. His cheeks had turned scarlet, as though his heart had rushed every last drop of blood in his body directly to his face.

"Right! That's it. The last bloody straw! Philip, you're not leaving this table until you've eaten every shitty mouthful on your plate, like the rest of us. Understood?"

Philip gazed at him with cool indifference. "Dead things can't go in dead things," he said. "Too much rot."

Father looked dumbfounded for a moment, before he sprang up from his chair, knocking over his glass of beer in the process, and launched himself at Philip on the opposite side of the table. Philip instinctively withdrew, alarmed by the speed of Father's advance, and Mother, squealing like a startled pig, flung out an arm to try and keep them apart; but Father was not to be deterred by such a feeble obstruction, and he violently pushed Mother's arm to one side. He grabbed Philip's left hand and guided it towards the plate, forcing him to scoop a chunk of sea bass onto the fork. He raised it towards Philip's mouth, holding his writhing head with his other hand and driving him towards the unappealing white meat.

"Eat it! Father shouted. "Eat the damn fish and be grateful. Be normal for once in your bloody life! Just once!"

Saul could hear Amy screaming "Stop it! Stop it!", her voice the terrified screech of a hunted animal, and from the corner of his eye he saw that Mother had been knocked from her chair and was now cowering on the carpet clutching her injured arm. Clearly Father, in his rage, had been unable to temper the force of his attack when Mother blindly attempted to intercede on Philip's behalf.

Saul watched it all unfold before him like a slow-motion ballet composition in a film. He rose to his feet and edged around the table. It was like moving through tar, impossibly dense and awkward, and in the time it took him to reach the grappling pair he saw Philip raise his hands to his face, heard him start to whimper like a frightened dog, noticed his eyes close and his head thrash from side to side as Father repeatedly drove at him with the fork.

"Eat the fucking fish!" Father screamed. "Please, Philip! Just one bite. For your mother and me."

He sounded desperate now, on the verge of an emotional collapse that Saul suspected might tip him over the edge for good. He took a second to look at his father—to really *see* him in this awful moment that was revealing him at his most pitiful, his most shameful—and he saw a man lost in a world of his own suffering, just as Philip was surely lost in his. He glanced down at the floor and saw Mother, helpless and hurt, staring up at Father with pale, humiliated eyes; in the distance he could still hear Amy sobbing, the noise cutting through Saul like the skirl of a chainsaw, as she begged her father to come to his senses and stop before Philip was hurt.

Saul took a deep breath, covered the distance between himself and his father with an agonizingly slow step, curled his fist, pulled back his arm, and struck the man he loved most in the world as hard as he could across the face. There was a moment of almost comical stillness—a nanosecond, no more—where the world stopped to process what Saul had done. Amy stopped crying; Mother looked on, her face flickering between confusion and shock; and Philip mirrored his brother exactly and watched Father topple to the floor, the fork and the chunk of sea bass no longer of any consequence at all.

The follow-through of Saul's swing almost threw him off balance and he was no more than a teetering gravitational blip away from joining his father on the floor. He caught himself just in time and placed a hand on the surface of the table. He was drawing in long, ragged breaths and felt light-headed, not so much from throwing the punch, but from seeing his father recoiling on the floor before him, staring up at him in disbelief. Saul felt disgusted, but he wasn't sure if it was with himself for striking a member of his family, or with his father for behaving so monstrously towards his son. It was probably a mixture of the two, but Saul was in no position to argue about which assumed the greater share. Instead, he simply stared at Father and tried hard not to vomit. He closed his eyes and listened to his frantic heartbeat. Each passing second brought a fresh wave of discomfort and shame.

"What have you done?" Mother said softly, sliding over towards Father on the floor. She made to place an arm around his shoulder, but he shrugged her off and scuttled towards the door; Saul could see the silver gleam of the fork on the carpet and the chunk of displaced sea bass no more than half a meter away from Father's hand. He stared at them both and frowned, trying to figure out how such savage violence could have been triggered by such a seemingly trivial domestic scene. It didn't make any sense; it was like a nightmare resolution to an innocent dream. His parents were both trembling on the floor, Philip and Amy were paralyzed with fear, and Saul felt utterly mortified that he had lost control. Blood was pounding in his head and he couldn't seem to think straight. The one thought that kept recurring was that, in the heat of a crisis, he and his father were essentially the same. What came naturally—no, *instinctively*—to both was violence.

Father turned and took one final look at Saul before dragging himself to his feet and leaving the room. In that look was everything Saul was afraid of; he could see right to the heart of his father's misery, where the true darkness had been in residence since Philip's change. Saul could already see the swelling below Father's right eye where his punch had landed, and he knew that their family would be transformed because of it.

Saul hung his head as Father left the room. He already regretted his actions, but the swelling would be a warning to Father that he could no longer treat Philip like a disobedient dog, not while Saul was around. Each time Father looked in the mirror he would see the bruise where Saul had hit him in his brother's defense; and somewhere in the bruise would dwell the sting from Saul's fist, a constant reminder of the hot blood that ran through the boy's veins, transporting him further and further away from his father's insurmountable grief.

For the rest of the night the house was silent. It felt to Saul like they were mourning the loss of a loved one and, in many ways, perhaps they were. Certainly there was no denying that the family dynamic had been transformed by the evening's events. Father had hidden himself away in the master bedroom and Mother occasionally checked in on him, unable to even look at Saul upon her return. Amy was downstairs watching television, while Mother spent several hours cleaning up the kitchen and finding odd jobs to occupy her mind. Philip had returned to his room and was poring over the disassembled components of the clock, still endeavoring to reverse time. Saul secretly wished him well, hoping that, tonight of all nights, the mystery might be solved. The thought of spinning time's arrow and re-enacting the entire scene was a fantasy that glittered before him, impossibly close yet forever beyond his reach.

After a while, he retired to bed feeling exhausted and morose. He wanted to knock on Father's door and apologize, but he was afraid of what he might find. Instead, he buried himself under the cotton sheets and fell into a turbulent, unsettled sleep. He dreamed of beating Father to death with Philip's clock, before travelling back in time and doing the whole thing over again.

When Saul awoke in the morning, it felt like he'd hardly slept. Father had left the house early and Mother had taken Amy into town to buy her a new pair of shoes for school. The house was as silent as it had been the previous night, only this time it was because he had the place to himself. The mood of despondency that had clung to the house only twelve hours earlier had been aired out; Mother had been up at the crack of dawn scrubbing clean every room to make sure no trace of the sour atmosphere remained. Saul could smell a harsh combination of detergent and lemon Pledge, a smell he had associated with Mother for as long as he could remember.

He poured himself a bowl of cereal and glanced out of the kitchen window. He frowned, puzzled by the view. There was something on the step leading up to the door and Saul narrowed his eyes to confirm the sight. It looked like an old-fashioned sweet jar. It had a red plastic screw-on lid and was filled with murky water. Floating in the water were at least half a dozen dying fish.

He put down the bowl of cereal and went to open the back door. He looked down at the sweet jar and then scanned the near horizon, searching for Philip. He was nowhere to be seen. Saul pictured him ankle-deep in the nearby dyke, scooping up more fish to replace those that hadn't made it through the night.

"Jesus," he said. He lifted up the sweet jar and carried it into the house. He placed a towel on the worktop and set the container down, peering through the glass into the harrowing world of the fish. Philip had screwed on the red plastic lid, but had created a small crack in it, presumably with the tip of Saul's bradawl. Into the crack he had wedged the hollow plastic barrel of a Bic pen. It had been Philip's heartrending attempt at introducing oxygen to the fish he had rescued and now hoped to preserve in the jar.

Saul shook his head; he felt dizzy and a little sick. He stared at the fish in the container and counted seven gudgeon. They didn't look real; their ugly faces looked like fat childish thumbs that had been scribbled on with a marker pen to create bulging eyes and a wide, gaping mouth. A number of them were lying on their side at the bottom of the makeshift tank, silently waiting for their time in captivity to pass. Two of them had already died and had floated to the top of the jar.

Saul closed his eyes for a moment, and when he opened them again he saw Philip through the kitchen window, walking across the cobbled yard towards the house. When he walked through the door he looked first at Saul, then at the sweet jar containing the fish. He bore a look of exquisite agony on his face.

"I wanted to protect them," he said. "I didn't want them to get eaten like those fish last night." He peered into the glass jar and opened and closed his mouth. It looked like he was showing the dying fish how to breathe.

Saul sighed. He tried to imagine what it might be like to be Philip, just for a single day, and found he lacked the imagination to do even that. His brother was like a wooden board that had been warped by the rain; neither pressure nor prayer could set it true.

"These fish should be in the dyke, Philip, with running water. You can't keep them in a jar like this, even with an air hole. They need oxygenated water so they can breathe."

Philip stared at Saul with a look of detached simplicity. "I tried to help them," he said.

"I know you did. But sometimes you can try too hard." He pictured Father struggling to come to terms with Philip's condition, flailing around in a state of desperate confusion, never quite knowing the right thing to say. "Sometimes you can even make things worse."

"I wanted them to be safe, in their own world. Just like the boy in the Fade."

Saul paused and conjured up the image of Philip's drawing, still pinned to his bedroom wall: the empty landscape; the distant hills; the lonely boy.

"There's nothing wrong with wanting that, Philip. That's a good thing. It's just that the sweet jar isn't the right environment for the fish. It's a bad place."

Philip looked at him for a moment, his eyes glazed over as he rooted through a bright memory that might or might not have been real.

"The Fade can be a bad place, too," he said softly.

Saul waited, but Philip failed to elaborate. If anything he seemed to regret having spoken at all.

"What do you mean?"

Philip placed a hand against the cool surface of the glass jar and tried to will the fish back to life. He seemed agitated and was opening and closing his mouth with greater frequency. If he could he would have breathed life into every one of those damn fish. He just didn't know how.

"There's a man," he said. "He lives in the Fade too. His face is strange. Just a grey veil of skin stretched across his skull. His eyes look like holes cut into a mask and his mouth is shapeless and black."

Saul's brow creased as he tried to process the concept of such a man. The image wasn't something he was keen to dwell on.

"Who is he?"

Philip stopped rubbing the glass jar and turned to look at his brother. "I don't know. I call him Pappy, because he reminds me of Father when he's drunk. He always carries a brown sack. I think he's looking for someone."

Saul leant forward, intrigued. "Who?"

"I don't know. Maybe me; maybe the boy. Anyone disturbing the silence."

Saul smiled as a thought occurred to him and he touched his brother on the arm.

"You had a nightmare, that's all. All this stuff about Pappy, it isn't real, Philip. It just seems that way because you had a run-in with Father last night. Remember?"

Philip nodded, but remained unconvinced. His expression suggested he knew better. Saul thought he saw a fleeting look of pity pass before his brother's face, as though Saul's imagination had somehow failed him. It was a startling moment of revelation and Saul felt momentarily disturbed. Perhaps it was he who was living in the counterfeit world, and Philip who understood the true configuration of reality. Though the Fade seemed like a wild improbability, it was nothing more than an extension of his condition, a meeting point between illusion and truth. And if Philip, in all his glorious eccentricity, could be real, then so too could the fantasy world in which he occasionally chose to live.

He stared at his brother again and realized he was still gazing at the dying fish.

"Sometimes, when you take a thing out of its natural habitat, that thing loses the will to live. It's best to leave it where it belongs, Philip. Do you see?"

Philip said nothing. He took the jar and, balancing it precariously in his hands, turned and started walking from the house.

"Where are you going?" Saul said.

Philip walked purposefully towards the door. Without looking back, he said: "Burial."

Saul considered stopping him, but then decided to leave him to it. It was an important part of the process; if nothing else, the dead fish deserved to be returned to the earth.

Father dragged himself home just as it was turning dark. Without his presence around the house, the day had been pretty uneventful. Mother and Amy returned, laden down with bags, and Saul endured a fifteen minute, blow-by-blow account from Amy of everything she and Mother had bought and the tremendous savings they had made. Amy relished moments like this and Saul did his best to feign interest and apply a smile that he hoped looked suitably sincere. Mother unpacked the shopping and made Amy polish and buff her new school shoes. This was a common practice. Whenever Mother bought footwear from a store, they all knew they were in for a protracted period of compulsive polishing when she got home. No pair ever quite met the standards she expected of newly purchased shoes. Mother wasn't satisfied until she could see the shadowy outline of her own reflection. Even then she would mumble about inferior leather and the lost art of polishing. It was one of the many tiny quirks that Saul loved her for: that meaningless march towards perfection.

By the time Father drifted in, they had all settled into their evening routine. Dinner had been cooked and eaten, and Amy and Saul had washed the dirty dishes and reset the table. Mother had her feet up on the vinyl pouffe in the front room, eyes flickering as she watched TV. Philip was attending to whatever curiosity was currently preoccupying him upstairs. Mother had asked Saul to check up on him, ominous silence always triggering alarm bells in her head where Philip was concerned, and he reluctantly approached his brother's room. The incident with the dead fish in the glass sweet jar was still fresh in his mind; he'd had more than enough of Philip's craziness for one day. Saul pictured him lying on his bed listening to music on an iPod, like a regular kid, and the absurdity of the image made him smile. The day that Philip did anything as conventional as listening to music was the day Saul would seriously start to worry about his brother's mental health.

Philip's bedroom door was ajar and Saul peered around the jamb and looked in. As usual, he wasn't prepared for the strange sight that greeted him, though why this was still the case after so many months of abnormal behavior Saul couldn't quite reconcile, even to himself.

Philip was on his hands and knees, pawing at the unmade mattress on the bed. He had a flashlight in his hand. His bedding had been balled up and dumped in the middle of the room. He had ripped open the fabric protecting the mattress and was shining the torch into the cluster of exposed springs, peering intently at their strange design.

Saul entered the room and lowered himself onto the carpet. He stared into the coiled darkness of the mattress.

"What's in there?"

Philip glanced over at him and then turned back to his search. "I heard a noise. Like something crawling between the springs."

Saul sighed and prepared to rationalize yet another of Philip's paranoid delusions.

"I doubt there's anything in there, Philip. The space is too small. See?"

Philip shone the flashlight into the labyrinth of springs. His brow creased as he worked his eyes through the tangled metal, as though negotiating a labyrinth in a children's puzzle book. He was mesmerized by the intricacy of the construction before him, just as he had been with the inner workings of the clock; he was determined to discover what secret lay hidden in the heart of the maze.

"There's nothing there," Saul said. "Just metal and dust."

"I heard it," Philip said, pushing his face into the hole in the mattress. "It carried on all through the night. It sounded like rats making a nest."

Saul shivered. He wanted to pull Philip away from the bed, just in case his wild fancy happened to be true. Rats foraging in the mattress, giving birth to a blind, squealing litter while he slept. Jesus.

"There are no rats," he said. "You just heard the springs creaking in the night. That's all."

Philip said nothing; instead he continued to poke around with the flashlight in the wreckage of the torn mattress. Saul knew there would be no reasoning with him. Once he had the flesh of some crazy conviction between his teeth, Philip clung on with the tenacity of a rabid dog. He was like Father in this regard: stubborn, relentless, perversely willful.

"They must be hiding," Philip said. "Or hunting for food."

"Philip, you have to listen to me." Saul tugged on his brother's arm until he was staring into his curiously simple face. "There are no rats in the damn mattress! Understand? You have to stop this shit. You're driving everybody mental."

Philip studied him. His eyelids never blinked once. Saul thought it was like watching a frozen image on satellite TV, where the expression was permanently fixed until the unit was reset. He wondered what Philip was thinking, tried to imagine what was going on inside his head. He could have spent a year guessing and not come close, so uniquely layered was Philip's perception of the world.

Saul looked away, embarrassed that he had lost control of his emotions. He thought again of Father, exploding over the dinner table as Philip simulated gulping air like a fish. He stood up and quietly left the room. He spent the rest of the night thinking about the appalling cunning of rats.

When Saul went downstairs, he found Father in the kitchen nursing a mug of tea. He glanced up as Saul entered the room and looked uncomfortable. He lowered his eyes and sipped his drink. He looked a mess, Saul thought; tired, unkempt, ill-at-ease.

"What's your brother up to?" he said.

Saul crossed the room and reached for a mug from the tree. He made himself a coffee and propped himself against the breakfast bar.

"Better you don't know. It'll just make you angry again."

Father stared at Saul, allowing his son to see the self-disgust reflected in his eyes.

"About that..."

Saul cut him off. "It doesn't matter," he said. "I understand. We all do. He drives everyone bat shit from time to time."

Father continued to stare. "But that's just it. It does matter, Saul. *He* matters. I want you to understand that. I just..." He faltered for a moment and stared aimlessly into the mug, as though the answer to life's complexity could be found floating in the bitterness of the tea. Father hesitated, hoping that Saul might bail him out, but Saul kept quiet, waiting for Father to articulate whatever sentiment he had begun.

"I just find it hard," he concluded weakly. "Like it's part of a game. Something he's doing simply to annoy me. Does that make sense?"

Saul nodded, understanding Father's position completely. It's what they all felt, on occasion, when Philip was listing towards some inexplicable behavior. It was a natural reaction; no one could remain coolly detached from his ritualized nonsense forever. Saul had even seen Mother grow frustrated with him, which was a clear indicator of how impossible Philip could be. It was a commonly held belief that Mother had the patience of a saint and rarely expressed her anger, but when she did Saul made a habit of immediately vacating the room.

"I can't stop worrying about him, Saul. I'm terrified of what's going to happen next."

Saul glanced across at Father and saw that the man had tears in his eyes. This disturbed him more than the depth of emotion he was confessing to. Saul realized that Father was close to the breaking point and, worse still, it occurred to him that he had no idea what to do. In any other eventuality, the answer was always to bring Father another can of beer, and he made a half-hearted move towards the fridge. Father tracked his progress and, when Saul paused and gazed back at him, a look of troubled under-standing passed between them.

"What are you doing?" Father said.

"I thought you might be hungry. You didn't eat much last night."

Father gave a rueful smile. "Didn't drink much, either, if that's what you're thinking."

Saul said nothing. He studied Father closely and realized it had been a long time since he'd really looked at him, since he'd taken the time to see the tiny changes that had occurred to his features. The transformation hit Saul like a hammer blow to the gut: Father was growing old. His brow was creased with lines he couldn't remember seeing before, his cheeks were riddled with broken capillaries from the booze, and dark circles had appeared below his eyes. Saul's breath caught in his throat for a moment and he felt a sudden urge to rush to his father and embrace him. He imagined what it might feel like to bury his head against his chest and close his eyes, to wrap his arms around that heavy waist and squeeze until his arms grew sore. As he stood watching him, a peculiar look passed across Father's face, and Saul even considered doing it, just to see what kind of reaction it received; but then the opportunity was gone, and once again Father cut a distant figure: lonely, exhausted and afraid. The moment for Saul to ease some of his father's pain had passed.

"Funny thing is," Father said, looking across at him, "the bloody sea bass was dry." He chuckled under his breath and shook his head. "Not that your mother needs to know that."

There was a prolonged silence, during which Saul considered quietly retreating; the idea of floating away from his father and the family's ongoing problems was more appealing than Saul was prepared to admit. There was no denying that a small part of him could easily have abandoned his father to his prayers.

"Where did you go?" Saul said. "Mother was worried."

Father raised his head. He looked troubled, as though the notion of Mother's anxiety was just one more consequence to regret.

"I needed to clear my head. There was more black stuff in there than I could handle. I could feel it getting away from me."

Saul nodded, remembering the scene at the dinner table. He had seen the accretion of the black stuff behind his father's eyes; they all had.

"Perhaps you should be telling Philip all this," he said.

Father shook his head. "There's no point. He'll already have forgotten all about it. That's the real irony here, Saul. It's always the rest of the family that suffers. Philip floats on as though nothing has happened."

Saul made to protest, but realized that his father was right. For Philip, the cataclysm that had befallen the previous evening's family dinner would be nothing more than a distant memory, as difficult for him to accurately recall as it might be for Saul to remember a scene from a movie he'd watched as a small boy.

Saul sighed, momentarily envious of Philip's inconsistent memory. The image of his crazed father launching himself across the dinner table was seared onto his retinas. It was all he could see. He would have paid good money to have the entire memory extracted from the dark recess in which it had taken root. To be able to wash the image away, as Philip no doubt would, was a blessing beyond measure. For Saul the situation was different. He already knew that he would bear the trauma of his father's explosive reaction forever, that one sickening moment in time haunting him for the rest of his life.

"You can't let him get to you like that," Saul said. He felt helpless just saying such a thing, as though he were addressing a child with behavior issues, a demented kid whose Ritalin intake needed to be increased. "You have to let him know you're in control."

Father lifted his eyes; they looked hollow and unfamiliar, the eyes of a soldier broken by a long lost war.

"I don't know how anymore," he said. "I'm not even sure I ever did."

The rest of the night was quiet and uneventful. Father gradually eased his way back into the living room and he and Mother spent the remainder of the night talking. Saul, accustomed to the rhythm of his parents' reconciliation, took Amy by the hand and led her into the kitchen, where he supervised a chaotic baking spree until it was time for her to go to bed. Once she was settled, he returned to the kitchen and spent another hour clearing up the mess she'd made. He found the process cathartic, and he listened to the comforting sound of his parents talking in the adjacent room as he set about returning the kitchen to an acceptable state.

When he was finished he returned to the living room to discover Mother and Father watching the television. There was a contented silence between them that was as familiar as the dim wash of light from the butterfly lamp perched atop the credenza. Mother looked up and smiled as Saul walked in and Father acknowledged him with a grunt. Neither of them said a word, but Saul knew that some kind of temporary moratorium had been reached. Remarkably, there wasn't a single beer can in sight, and Saul quietly wondered how long his father's temperance might last. That he had foresworn the booze even for a night was worthy of celebration, and Saul nodded at his father and kissed his mother on the top of the head as he walked past. They were all due a change in fortune; maybe this was where their break would begin.

Saul ascended the stairs feeling emotionally and physically drained. It had been an exhausting twenty-four hours and he could feel his body starting to shut down. The lids of his eyes felt heavy; his breathing was controlled and slow.

He stepped onto the landing and glanced across at Philip's bedroom door. As always, it was open. Mother had insisted on this being the case ever since Philip had been diagnosed with Cotard's syndrome. She and Father clambered out of bed and checked up on him at least half a dozen times during the night. Peering through the door at three a.m. was their safety valve; they could sleep easily again having seen their son's face in the pale green glow of the Kermit the Frog night light.

Saul paused a moment and stole a glance through the open door. He could see the rim of Philip's skull, flickering by the green light of Kermit's grin, seeming to pulse with a strange alien sheen.

He could hear his brother's erratic breathing and caught a glimpse of a complex network of toilet tissue and paper that Philip had crammed inside his mattress, presumably in an attempt to prevent the rats from having a free run at him during the night.

His eyes drifted towards the wall above the bed and settled on Philip's drawing of the Fade. With the faint green aura enveloping it, it looked even more surreal than Saul remembered. He made to turn away and then stopped, frowning, having caught sight of something in the green shadows of the newly layered landscape of the Fade. He leant forward and peered into the green haze of Philip's room. The drawing seemed to shimmer, appearing to invite him closer, and he moved across the landing, opened the door, and silently made his way into Philip's room. He glanced down at his brother, anxious not to disturb him. If Philip awoke to discover a dark shape hovering over him, the consequences would be harrowing beyond belief.

Saul carefully approached the picture and stared hard at the shaded hills in the background. Could he see the weirdly config-ured outline of a man pressed up against the rock, his body seeming to melt into the shadows? He stepped closer and nudged Philip's bed with his leg. He leaned in, but to no avail. The image retreated. He was too close to the picture. The outline he thought he'd seen was now just a random scribble of graphite on the page. He withdrew slowly, keeping his eyes on the ridges and slopes of the hills. When his face was about two feet away from the image, he stopped. There it was again: a distinct shape pressed against the rock. Saul narrowed his eyes and held his breath as he stared. The drawing rewarded him with a blurry impression of a thin man, barely visible in the distance, and almost impossible to differen-tiate from the dark profile of the rocks. Saul squinted his eyes and pressed his retinas to even greater labor. The man seemed to be holding something in his right hand. It looked to Saul like it could have been a large sack, but he was conscious of what Philip had told him earlier in the day. Could he simply be creating something out of nothing, based solely on Philip's crazy story of a man named Pappy? He recalled his brother telling him: *His face is strange. Just a grey veil of skin stretched across his skull. His eyes look like holes cut into a mask and his mouth is shapeless and black.*

Saul felt a sudden chill and shook his head, trying to dislodge the notion of the faceless man lurking in the shadows. He took two steps back and reassessed the drawing from a different perspective. The thin man in the rocks had disappeared. If he was there at all, his outline had become just another sweeping abstraction, reclaimed by the dark cradle of the hills. All he could see was the strange landscape that he'd seen previously, now oddly illuminated, showing him the lonely boy, the scarred earth, the distant shore.

Saul turned away, deeply troubled, and listened to Philip breathing steadily beneath the sheets. As he left the room, he imagined the thin man with no face lurking in the Fade, poised directly above his brother's head, swinging an empty sack in the dim green light of Kermit the Frog's insatiable grin.

8

PAPPY

Deep inside the barn, bound hand and foot in the straw-filled mezzanine, David silently beheld the Fade. His eyes were wide and he felt sick to the stomach as the place revealed itself as a flickering grey aberration, an improbable reality somehow overlaying the physical plane of existence that his mind insisted must still be there. He squinted hard and could just about make out the warped boards and shifting shadows of the barn, trembling at the very edge of his vision, fluttering beneath the Fade, as though viewed through a prism of water.

By contrast, the vast space of Hilary Bunce's miracle retreat spread before him like a coded message waiting to be cracked. The world of the barn and the ice cream van and the kidnapping had been left behind; here was a place of brooding emptiness, where time had been hollowed out and the urgency of living transformed into a solemn moment of anticipation, stretched out forever in the Fade.

David peered into the empty landscape and felt like a small child abandoned in the middle of nowhere. The grey dust of the valley stretched for miles either side of him and vast hills rolled their shoulders across a leaden sky. In the distance, the horizon changed color and he thought he could see a pale shore, with a slate-grey sea beyond. He narrowed his eyes and held his breath. Amid the terrifying stillness of the Fade, there was movement: a frail figure darting in and out of the heavy shadows of the hills. David watched carefully, trying to gauge whether or not it would be safe to shout for help. The figure was moving swiftly, as though completely at ease in the place, and David momentarily wondered if it could be Bunce. He stared hard and instantly realized his mistake. The figure was too small to be Bunce, even taking into account the distance between them, which meant it had to be someone else. David felt a sudden rush of euphoria. He was so overwhelmed by the possibility of freedom, he felt on the verge of tears. If the figure wasn't Bunce, then the Fade was not the private kingdom his captor imagined it to be. There was another. And where there was one, David thought, there could quite easily be two. He felt such a surge of triumph at the prospect of giving Bunce the slip that he had to look twice when a second figure detached itself from the shadows and shuffled forward from a cleft in the hills. David froze and looked on, mesmerized. The second figure was tall and impossibly thin and, though it was some distance behind the first figure, was clearly in active pursuit. It clung to the black hills as though it were well acquainted with the darkness in which it hid. There was something not quite right with the figure's composition, as though its anatomy had been strangely distorted, and David felt a chill deep in the marrow of his bones. He realized with a suddenness that robbed him of all hope that if the second figure ever discovered he was there, it would never allow him to leave.

He flattened himself against the ground and watched the silent pursuit across the grey landscape. A subtle dread had replaced any feelings he'd had of finding a possible ally. He peered across the desolate valley and stared hard at the irregular movements of the thin man. He was carrying an empty sack in his left hand, David noticed, swinging it freely as his black boots kicked up tiny explosions of dust. He looked totally at peace with himself, lost in the simple rhythms of his undertaking. Like a man conforming to a preordained destiny; a faceless agent of fear.

———

Hilary Bunce was seated at the kitchen table eating a breakfast of cereal and hot toast. When Pa walked in he uttered a grunt that Bunce assumed to be a greeting and seated himself in the chair opposite. He opened his newspaper and buried his head in the grim turmoil of world affairs.

Bunce continued to eat and stared at Pa's large hands, spread either side of the paper. The fingers looked strong and were deeply grained with the ancient signature of the sun and the earth. He remembered them wrapped around Ma's slender waist, when the family had still been together and the world had been a brighter place; but the image quickly vanished, barely even formed before it had been replaced by the memory of Ma's finger buried in the jewelry box out in the woods. It sprang at him like a beacon, hypnotizing him for a moment, forcing him to consider for the thousandth time the possible sequence of events that had led to Ma's death. He suspected he'd never know, not completely; the past had devoured the moment and the horror of it lay buried beneath countless layers of his father's lies. To solve the riddle of why Ma's wedding finger had been removed and placed in an illicit shrine beneath the earth he would have to delve deep into Pa's broken psyche, and such a thing was never likely to come to pass. Bunce shuddered at the mere thought of it; even now, he could barely bring himself to look Pa in the eye.

He stood up and made Pa some coffee and a bowl of cereal. He placed both the mug and the bowl beside the newspaper and Pa emitted another grunt without looking up. Bunce sat back down at the table and silently resumed eating his breakfast. The room felt like a temple, Bunce thought, as though a moment of somber prayer had been captured in the stillness; then his mind flipped the notion and it occurred to him that the room was more like a morgue, devoid of intimacy and possessed only by the memory of the recent dead. He smiled at the extreme contrast of the image: temple and morgue; salvation and decay. How bittersweet life could be, even in unremarkable moments such as this. He glanced at his father over the bowl of cereal and watched him read. Pa was perfectly still. It was like trying to detect movement in the minute hand of a clock; Bunce knew Pa's body must be subtly shifting, he just couldn't see the muscles working with the naked eye.

It was at that point that Fliss and Gilly breezed into the kitchen, Gilly freshly shaven and ready for war, as always, Fliss throwing back her hair and chuckling at a private joke. Pa looked up and stared at them. He seemed disappointed with himself for having done so. His expression remained flat and empty, as though Fliss and Gilly were just another tragic news story to be glossed over during an uneventful breakfast.

"What's so funny?" he said, almost inaudibly.

Fliss glanced over at him and Bunce thought it was at precisely this moment that she realized she had made a terrible mistake. Pa knew everything. She could see the hurt and rage reflected in his eyes. Bunce smiled as he saw the realization creep across Fliss's face. There was a brief flash of panic in her eyes, and then a formidable look of defiance that Bunce knew all too well. She drew in a deep breath and held Pa's gaze for what seemed like an unnaturally long time.

"Gilly made a joke," she said. "Did it disturb his Highness's breakfast?"

Gilly stifled a laugh as he reached into the cupboard for a mug. Bunce waited and watched.

"What was it?" Pa said.

Fliss seated herself at the table and frowned. "Pardon?"

"The joke. What was it that Gilly said that made you laugh? I'd like to hear it."

There was another lengthy silence; another flash of fear in Fliss's eyes. She had underestimated Pa and was only now beginning to regret her miscalculation. She had failed to factor in the pain and the shame and the grief he had been battling with ever since Ma's passing. She had taken him for a fool when he was clearly anything but; Bunce could have told her that, had she been prudent enough to ask. Fliss would be wise now to show humility and remorse. Pa already knew the worst of it. He could see it in the woman's dark, disdainful eyes. The sickening betrayal that Bunce had alluded to the previous night was all too apparent in Fliss's mocking gaze and Pa could see the contempt in which she now held him. The thread that had just about held them together for the last few months was finally beginning to fray.

"It was nothing," she said. "Just a silly little joke. Jesus, Bill, what the hell's got into you this morning?"

Pa folded his newspaper and directed his full attention towards Fliss. "I like a good laugh," he said. "Maybe I'll find it funny too. Why don't you try me?"

The tension in the room intensified; Bunce sat with his spoon raised midway to his mouth, suddenly afraid to move.

"All I said was—" Gilly began, but Pa silenced him with an icy glare.

"Keep quiet, lad. I don't want to hear it from you. I want to hear it from her."

For all Gilly's obscene bravado, he knew when to keep his counsel, especially when Pa sounded so fiercely determined.

Pa stared at Fliss and waited.

"The joke," he said.

She paused for a moment, glancing round the room; she briefly settled on Hilary Bunce's moon of a face, before moving on and returning to Pa.

"If you must know," she said, "we were laughing at you. At how stupid you must be to be so unaware of what's going on under you own damn roof." She was almost radiant with spite and defiance. "Happy now?"

Pa nodded slowly and Bunce thought he looked uncommonly sad, like an alien suddenly stranded far from home.

"Oh, I know exactly what's going on," he said, turning his sorrowful gaze upon Gilly. "I've known for some time. I just wasn't sure what to do about it."

Gilly's face turned pale and he stared at his father with an expression that looked to Bunce like an unhappy fusion of horror and humiliation.

"How typical," Fliss said. "As indecisive as ever, even when confronted with a crisis." She emitted a snort of derision. "You're weak and pathetic, Bill, just like him." She pointed at Bunce, who froze under Fliss's withering gaze.

Gilly took a step forward and made to speak, but Pa held up his hand.

"Let her speak, son," he said. "I suspect she has a little more to say, don't you, Fliss?"

Her face turned scarlet, irritated by Pa's controlled tone, the easy manner with which he seemed to be accepting her infidelity.

"What's left to say?" she added, her voice rising slightly. "I fucked your son, Bill. Is that what you want to hear? I fucked your son while you were down here eating your toast and reading the newspaper. That's what we were laughing at. Okay? That's what we found so fucking amusing. That your son's cock was inside me while you were busy dunking your toast."

Bunce threw back his chair and stood up, towering over the table.

"Don't talk to him like that!" he screamed. "*Don't you fucking dare!*"

He drew back his arm, weighted it with all the bitterness and rage of a thousand unpleasant days in Fliss's company, and swung it hard towards the woman's face. Fliss had but a second to acknowledge with some degree of surprise that the fist was going to knock her unconscious, before the bones in Bunce's hand and those in Fliss's jaw connected. The force of the punch was such that it knocked her off the chair and sent her reeling backwards, where she cracked her head hard on the tiled floor.

By this stage Pa had risen to his feet and Gilly was already leaning forward to tend to Fliss. Bunce was lost in the moment, frozen by the sense of outrage that had overwhelmed him, barely even aware of what he'd done.

Pa stepped forward and spoke firmly to Gilly. "Don't touch her," he said. "We need to take a minute to think things through."

"What's to think about? She's out cold. He might even have killed her."

Pa said nothing and Gilly glanced up at him and then quickly turned away.

"Look at me, Gilly." When his son had summoned the courage to do so, Pa continued. "You need to consider where your loyalties lie. Okay? Are they with the family? Or are they with her?" He glanced down at the body of Fliss; a small pool of blood had begun to form at the crown of her head. "Forgiveness comes easy, son, if you repent. You just have to take the first step."

Pa smiled at Gilly, who nodded, glanced across at Bunce, and then stepped cleanly away from the body, his journey of redemption begun.

The three of them stood in the kitchen forming a rough screen around the fallen body of Fliss. They were watching the pool of blood at her crown expand across the tiles. Pa stared, mesmerized, as it tracked along the smooth runnels of grout and seeped across the surface of the floor. It was a protracted moment of almost absurd proportions, like staring down from an airplane at the diminished land below. It felt to Pa like he was watching a documentary on TV, the scene before him cold, distant, unreal. He imagined Fliss's slack face pixelating and breaking up into scraps of nothingness if he got too close, like an image on a flickering screen.

Beside him Bunce was breathing hard and his hand, still clenched into a tight fist, was trembling. The evidence of what he'd just done lay before him, but Bunce thought Fliss looked like a broken puppet, sprawled awkwardly in a puddle of fake blood as part of some grand scheme to get him into trouble with Pa. He panted like a dazed animal in the silence, trying to still his thundering heart, and considered the possible consequences if Fliss turned out to be dead. A thin smile spread across his face; the prospect filled him with an emotion he could barely describe. Not so much happiness, as exultation. He looked across at Pa and Gilly and wanted to reassure them, wanted to let them know that soon enough the family would once again be at peace. If Fliss was dead, it didn't matter. He could clean up his own mess, he was sure of it. He knew a way. He just needed a little help fitting together the pieces.

He glanced across at Gilly, who, of the three of them, was clearly the most distressed. His eyes looked wild and his face was as pallid as the underside of a flayed trout. The woman he had been fucking no more than twenty minutes earlier was now lying at his feet, staring at the ceiling, seeing nothing. For all his talk of "mission focus" and being "outside the wire", Gilly looked like a man in conflict with himself, torn between the horror of his new reality, and the knowledge that at some point he would have to come face to face with his Pa. When all this had died down, his betrayal would still exist, and he was already considering the toll to both himself and his father, no matter how much Pa said he was prepared to forgive. He stared at Fliss's unmoving body and silently wondered how long it would be before his father would be able to trust him again.

Pa stepped forward, lowered himself over Fliss's outstretched legs, and felt for a pulse. He looked over his shoulder at Bunce.

"She's gone," he said. "I guess we ought to do something."

Gilly stared hard at Bunce, his own fists opening and closing in a pale imitation of his brother's rage. "Look what you've done," he said. "What the hell were you thinking?"

For once Bunce stood his ground; he returned Gilly's grim look of open hostility.

"I could ask you the same thing," he said quietly.

Gilly bristled at the underlying accusation. "What the fuck's that supposed to mean?" He took a step forward and only reconsidered when Pa held up a hand and stopped him in his tracks.

"Another time, maybe," he said. "We have enough to contend with right here. Gilly, I want you to clean up the kitchen and pack all of Fliss's things into a suitcase. Okay?"

Gilly made to protest, but the uncompromising resolve in Pa's eyes checked his tongue. Instead, he lowered his head and nodded, trying not to imagine how grotesque it would be to trawl through his dead lover's wardrobe before the day had barely begun.

"Hilary, you and I will have to bury the body. I know it's a terrible thing, but it has to be done, okay? Do you think you can manage that?"

Bunce hesitated, realizing he was on the verge of disclosing his only real secret in the world. It could be done, he knew it could, but he wasn't sure he wanted Fliss's body turning to dust in the one place that he cherished above all others.

"We can do it in the woods," Pa was saying, "at the back of the house. I know a good spot where the soil's soft."

Bunce knew exactly where he meant; he had seen it with his own eyes. He pictured Pa's hands lifting the stone altar and raising the wooden box containing Ma's finger, the wedding band anointed by the dim light filtering through the canopy of trees.

He looked across at Pa and shook his head. "Not there. It's too public." He had expected to be silenced even before he'd opened his mouth, but Pa watched him and waited, the trauma of the morning's events plain to see in the man's gaunt, exhausted face.

Bunce smiled and reached out to take Pa's hand. "There's somewhere better," he said.

Bunce had anticipated opposition, if not from Pa, who was starting to look increasingly spent, then from Gilly, whose resistance to any plan proposed by Bunce seemed to be an automatic condition of their relationship. Before a word could be exchanged, however, Pa ordered Gilly upstairs to begin clearing out Fliss's wardrobe. He then nodded towards Bunce, seemingly content to allow him to assume control of a situation he had recklessly created. They retrieved a large tarpaulin from the back of Pa's truck and returned to the kitchen. Gilly had vacated the room and they stood staring at Fliss's neglected body, both feeling uneasy in the silence.

Bunce stared at Fliss and remembered that slack, dead face screaming abuse at him. How helpless she looked now, he thought; how impossibly fragile and small. Had that broken body really contained so much bile? A thought suddenly occurred to him: if she had haunted him so cruelly while alive, how much worse might it be now? Would she return, her face bruised and yellow, the back of her head caved in from the fall, wailing along the empty corridors of the house, desperate to shed his family's blood?

He shook the notion from his head and glanced across at Pa, who was also staring down at the forlorn body, no doubt battling his own demons, looking for ways to combat the guilt that he knew would be waiting for him as he lay awake in the dead of night.

"Why did they do it?" he said. The question was muttered under his breath and was almost inaudible, but Bunce heard it clearly enough and felt the intensity of his father's pain. There was no easy answer, of course, and so he remained silent. Pa would never be able to work out why Fliss had seen the need to seduce his eldest child; it wasn't like figuring out an equation, where a solution could be reached simply by applying the correct formula. This was more complicated, more irrational, like trying to fit a circle perfectly inside a square. All he had to work with were Fliss's final words, announcing the chilling reality of her betrayal, which Bunce knew would live with his father forever: *I fucked your son while you were down here eating your toast and reading the newspaper. That's what we were laughing at... That's what we found so fucking amusing. That your son's cock was inside me while you were busy dunking your toast.*

Pa spent another moment staring at Fliss's unmoving body; he vaguely wondered what would happen to all the blood floating inside her veins now that the thing designed to keep the stuff pumping had ground to a halt. Turn to mush, he supposed, just like the rest of her. He looked up and caught Bunce staring at him.

"This place of yours," he said. "Is it far away?"

Bunce shook his head. "Closer than you might think."

Pa nodded again and indicated for Bunce to help him unfold the tarpaulin and spread it out on the kitchen floor besides Fliss's corpse. He gestured for Bunce to take the shoulders, while he took hold of the dead woman's feet.

"On three," he said. He counted them in and he and Bunce lifted the body onto the tarpaulin. They shuffled it into the middle of the dark fabric and bound it tightly until the body was no longer visible. That simple, Bunce thought, warding off a shudder. He peered at the dark stain on the kitchen floor where Fliss's head had cracked open and then glanced down at the shapeless weight wrapped inside the tarpaulin. A woman's life reduced to nothing more than what had spilled out and what could be trussed up; even to Bunce, it felt somehow tragic, a moment of heartbreaking revelation.

"You ready for this?" Pa said, breaking Bunce's private deliberation.

Bunce nodded. He stepped beyond the tarpaulin and opened the kitchen door. Outside, the air felt fresh; the sky was clear and empty of clouds, a surreal, penetrating blue. He returned to the kitchen and followed Pa's lead, bending low to lift the tarpaulin. Once they were comfortable with its weight, they carried it out into the cobbled yard.

"We loading it on the truck?" Pa said.

Bunce shook his head. "No need. The place I have in mind is nearer than you think."

Pa paused for a moment and stared across the strange space that separated them, the two connected by the grisly bridge of the sagging tarpaulin.

"This is important, Hilary. We can't afford any more mistakes, okay? Perhaps you ought to tell me what you have in mind."

Bunce smiled at his father's misgivings. "It's fine, Pa. You have to trust me. I have the perfect place. No one will ever find her there, I promise."

Pa watched him for a moment, then nodded. Of all his family, Hilary was the only one that he had always implicitly trusted. He had his failings, true enough, but then who among them could consider themselves faultless? Hilary was slow and awkward and often careless, but he was also devoted to his family, loyal to the bitter end. Did that not, in the final reckoning, outweigh all else? To Pa's way of thinking it had to; when the rapture was visited upon them, it would be the loyal and the dutiful that would rise up first. If that were the case, Pa thought, then only Hilary could be said to be truly worthy of the call.

Pa searched Bunce's face and saw only a guileless desire to please. He smiled and said: "I believe you, lad."

They tightened their grip on the tarpaulin and Bunce led them over the cobbled yard towards the barn. They made their way inside, struggling with the large door, and Bunce guided them towards the mezzanine. When they reached the ladder, Pa stopped and sighed.

"It's a nice idea, Hilary, but this is too close to home. We can't leave the body up there. The smell will be unbearable."

"It not what it seems, Pa. Okay? You have to have a little faith. Just a little."

Pa blew heavily through his teeth and winced as he helped heave the body in the tarpaulin across Bunce's left shoulder.

"If this turns out to be some wild goose chase, Hilary, I'll be mad as hell. You understand?"

"It's not," Bunce said. "Just stand clear, then follow me up. You'll see."

Pa did as he'd been instructed, winding his way up the ladder to the mezzanine, watching Bunce's large frame hoist the tarpaulin into the upper part of the barn with ease and then looking about in surprise, as though something was amiss.

Pa followed his gaze, taking in the skewed bed of straw and disjointed beams. Bunce's face had turned pale and he was looking about the empty mezzanine with increasing consternation. His eyes were tearing at the emptiness, looking for whatever damn fool thing he thought he'd lost, panic spreading across his features, separating his lips and revealing bared teeth as yellow as week old smog.

Pa stepped up into the mezzanine and frowned at his son's growing alarm. "Whatever it is, you won't find it up here," he said. "Place has been nothing but straw for years."

Bunce turned to his father and held his breath.

"There's a boy," he said. His eyes were still darting round the mezzanine. "I left him right here."

Pa's frown had deepened. "What in hell's name are you talking about, lad?"

Bunce was down on his knees now, poring through the straw, and Pa grabbed him by the arm and hauled him to his feet. There was a steely resilience in the man's gaze, but inside he felt hollow, as though the very marrow of his being had worked itself loose. Bunce's words were pounding in his head, as though they'd been driven into his skull with a mallet: *There's a boy. I left him right here*; words that, though innocent enough when taken on their own terms, filled him with a nameless dread. He heard them again and again and a part of him suspected the worst; in truth, he had been waiting to hear this kind of chilling admission for some time.

"You're talking in riddles, Hilary. Just stop for a minute and tell me what the devil's going on."

Bunce stared into his father's eyes, and Pa could see the fear and the desperation lodged deep within. He looked just as he had as a small child when he knew he'd done something wrong and was waiting for Pa to administer the strap.

"It's pointless trying to explain," Bunce said. "It's better if I just show you."

He stooped down towards the tarpaulin and placed one hand

firmly on the curved ridge of Fliss's hidden body. He looked up and urged his father to follow his example.

"What is this nonsense?" Pa said. He had taken a step back towards the ladder and his anger was evident in the color rising on his cheeks. Bunce could see that Pa was only seconds away from disciplining him and he hesitantly reached for his father's hand.

"Please, Pa. It'll just take a second. You have to trust me."

Pa briefly flirted with the idea of abandoning his son to whatever craziness seemed to have claimed him. He gazed at Bunce's outstretched hand and remembered how small it had felt when he used to hold it, Hilary no more than a small boy, shadowing him on the farm. The memory was enough to allow him to see something of the boy still alive in the young man kneeling before him, and he slowly reached out and waited for Bunce, whose hand was now bigger than his own, to complete the ritual. Bunce smiled and drew his father towards the tarpaulin. Pa had to stoop to accommodate the movement and Bunce heard his knees crack as he knelt over the covered mound of Fliss's corpse. Bunce eased Pa's hand onto the tarpaulin and then placed his own palm on top of it; he could feel the cool bones of his father's knuckles beneath his fingers.

"I've never done it like this before," he said. "It might take a while."

But to Bunce's surprise, the migration from the barn to the Fade was almost instantaneous. Perhaps it was because of the emotional flux he was experiencing, or the arcane transference of power between father and son; it was hard to tell. All Bunce could ascertain in the strange skirl of the crossing was that his father and the tarpaulin-covered body of Fliss had both made the journey intact.

Bunce braced himself and caught his father by the hand as the capricious nature of the Fade established itself around them. He watched Pa's eyes widen as he tried to process the pale blue wash that engulfed them. He looked like a man who had been plunged into a new element, and Bunce held onto him as Pa gasped for air and stared into the impossible wilderness that stretched beyond the barn.

"What in God's name—" he began, but then trailed away, losing the thread of the simplest sentence in the enormity of what lay around him.

"It's called the Fade," Bunce said softly. "It's where I come sometimes to escape."

Pa stared at the blue fringe of light that fluttered at the border of his newly-mutated perspective. He looked stunned, as though his entire belief system had collapsed, leaving only the wreckage of some nightmare vision in its place.

"I can still see the barn," he muttered, "but I can also see..." He broke off and looked across at Bunce, defying him to question his sanity. "Do you see it?" he said. "The grey desert, the hills...Tell me you see it too!"

Bunce smiled. "I see it, Pa. I've always seen it." He looked out across the empty plain and felt a deepening sense of unease. He still couldn't see the boy. He cast his mind back to the last time they'd been together. He had left David struggling to come to terms with the arid vistas of the Fade. He had abandoned him there, bound hand and foot, held captive by his own rising terror. Even if he'd been able to unshackle himself, Bunce thought, where could he possibly have gone? Venturing deeper into the Fade would only lead him further from the barn, which remained his only connection to the distant suburban street he called home. David didn't seem like the kind of boy who was foolish enough to sacrifice whatever hope he had left for the sake of a little curiosity. With each footstep he took, the blue radiance of the barn would have diminished, until the only guiding light that remained would have been the gunmetal streaks in the sky. The Fade was not a place that solicited tourism. It was Hilary Bunce's private kingdom, born in the blackened rubble of his imagination. This is how Bunce had always thought of the place, and it would serve David well to think this way too. Otherwise, who knew what might happen to him? Not even Bunce knew what stillborn forms clung to the shadows beneath the hills.

He looked back at his father, who was still fiercely gripping his hand, and said: "See, Pa. The perfect spot. Just like I told you."

Pa slowly released Bunce's hand and rose to his feet. He stared at the blue light wrinkling the edges of the mezzanine, then peered out across the Fade, looking thoughtful.

"Who knows about this place?" he said.

Bunce met Pa's gaze and felt his heart flutter. As ever the old man had cut straight to the heart of the matter, despite his ambivalence about the Fade's configuration. Bunce could see in Pa's eyes that the provenance of his son's secret kingdom profoundly troubled him, but he was still shrewd enough to realize that the Fade—whatever the hell it was—might very well be the ideal resting place for Fliss.

Bunce stood up and towered over his father, trying to conceal any hint of frailty.

"The Fade belongs to me," he said possessively. "No one knows."

Pa stepped forward, feeling the hot brush of desert sand beneath his feet instead of straw.

"Then who's the boy?"

Bunce felt himself shrink inside his skin; the cheeks of his moon face turned red.

"What boy?"

Pa stared at him. "The one you were looking for when you first entered the barn, lad."

Bunce shuffled, not knowing what to say, not knowing how

best to explain the situation that had developed with the missing boy.

"Come on, Hilary," Pa said. "Don't take me for a bloody fool. I think we're a little past all that now, don't you?"

Bunce closed his eyes for a moment and David's terror-stricken face rose up to meet him, still dripping blood from where Bunce had ripped out the silver pin above his eye.

"He's just a kid," Bunce said. "He's not important."

Pa reached out and laid a rough hand across Bunce's left arm.

"Not good enough," Pa said. "What was he doing in the barn in the first place?"

Bunce hesitated, then looked away. His throat felt dry; he was struggling to find the right words, *any* words, the process of trying to articulate his relationship with the boy squeezing the insides of his skull.

"I brought him here," Bunce began.

Pa nodded encouragement. "Why?"

"He was mean to me. I wanted to teach him a lesson. I took him off the street and placed him in the Fade. I wanted him to know what it felt like to be totally alone."

Pa closed his own eyes for a moment, feeling a sudden spasm in his chest.

"Jesus, Hilary. You kidnapped him?"

Bunce shook his head firmly. "I just…" His voice trailed off, before a thought occurred to him: "I just wanted him to stop saying mean things."

Pa blew air through his cheeks and gazed out at the untrammeled country Bunce had somehow created.

"So what happened to him?" he said. He looked again at the wilderness of desert and the darkening slopes of the hills. "Where the devil is he?"

Bunce lowered his head. "He should be right here. I left him tied up, Pa, hands and feet. I don't understand…" He peered around wildly to see if there were any footprints in the sand, but the wind had made a mockery of the canvas, leaving only a featureless expanse of endlessly spiraling dust.

Pa breathed slowly, fighting the urge to throttle the life from his troubled son. He vaguely wondered what other sad narratives were stored inside Hilary's head.

"So at least three people know about this place," Pa said. "The two of us and the missing boy."

Bunce nodded. He looked utterly dejected, as though the confidence he had felt earlier had been slowly pumped out of him.

"We can also assume," Pa went on, "that either this boy has the skills of Houdini, or else he has been located and set free by a third party. Would this be a fair assessment of the situation as we understand it, Hilary?"

Another nod from Bunce, this time accompanied by a solitary, heaving sob; Pa looked up and clipped him round the head, hard enough to make Bunce lose his footing in the sand.

"None of that, lad. We've enough to deal with right here without you bursting a pipe. There'll be plenty of time for tears later. I daresay I'll join you, when the time's right, but not now. Okay?"

Bunce sniffed and wiped his nose on the sleeve of his shirt. Pa's clout to the head had sent another jolt of pain racing around his skull; he could barely think in a straight line anymore. All he wanted to do was lie down in the Fade and disappear, just like he'd always been able to. He suddenly realized what a terrible mistake he'd made introducing the boy and Pa to his private kingdom. The place was no longer his own. He had opened the door to others and foolishly invited them in. He would pay a heavy price for such carelessness. The Fade would find a way of punishing him for his indiscretion; it might even rob him of the right to enter the place as he pleased.

"We have to find him," Bunce said. "The boy. He could be anywhere."

Pa smiled, but Bunce realized there was no humor in it, only a steely resilience to assimilate the new environment into which he had been cast. Pa was already adapting to the idiosyncrasies of the Fade's geography, thinking ahead, refining his strategy, his eyes mapping the horizon beyond the dunes.

"He's the least of our worries right now," he said, staring down at the body wrapped in the tarpaulin. "Our priority is Fliss. We have to find somewhere safe to ditch the body. Somewhere remote."

He pointed to the shadowy declension of the grey slopes.

"That looks perfect," he said. "We'll head there. I'll secure the tarpaulin and you can drag it along the sand."

Bunce said nothing, but a knot began to form in his stomach. He didn't know why, but the hills had always frightened him. He had never ventured too close, preferring instead to explore the desert and the far-flung shore. He had always imagined that if the Fade carried any kind of threat, it would be most concentrated in the creeping influence of the hills.

He glanced across at Pa again and watched as he stared wistfully at the haunting terrain.

"What is this place?" he said softly, almost to himself. "I've never seen anything like it. Is it even real?"

Bunce remained silent, sensing that his father wasn't expecting a response; but it was real alright, and he could feel it slipping away. The covenant he had established with the Fade was no longer his alone. There were intruders, spoiling its beauty, their presence infecting the land. Bunce felt his heart thunder inside his chest as an idea began to form; he knew what had to be done. To reclaim the Fade would require a measured violation; to wit, he was almost instantly decided: he would spill blood beneath the watchful gaze of the hills.

9

NEST

David watched the two figures for some time, one shadowing the other, until eventually both disappeared behind the dunes. He wanted to call out to the boy in front, but his fear of the thin man trailing him was too great. He was only able to isolate him against the dark backdrop of the hills intermittently, but each time he caught sight of him, he felt a constriction in his chest and his breath grew increasingly labored. He wanted to alert the boy to the thin man's presence, wanted to scream at him to take whatever drastic action was necessary, but his throat was dry and he was terrified of declaring his own position. It felt like he was fighting too many complex emotions: a desperate desire to summon help; anxiety for the boy being pursued across the grey desert; a mounting sense of unassailable dread. There was a dull ache at the back of his head from trying to reconcile the hope and fear raging inside.

He shuffled lower in the sand, trying to keep himself out of sight. The twine binding his hands and feet was cutting into his flesh; the left side of his face throbbed, a distant reminder of where Bunce had ripped the silver pin from his brow. His whole body felt raw, as though it had been stripped down to the very sinews, exposing every nerve cluster to the biting desert wind. He tried to remember what he had done to deserve such a fate, and the vile words he had spat at Bunce as he tried to make a meager living in the ice cream van came rushing back at him: *dirty bastard, fat cunt, fucking pervert.* He could still feel a little of the poison running through his veins, and the image of Bunce in his apron serving at the van's hatch made him feel sick. He grimaced and shook his head. That Fate might have delivered him here as an act of justifiable retribution never once occurred to him. His toxic treatment of Bunce was easily rationalized by the man's subsequent abduction of him. Bunce had behaved according to David's sour opinion of him; he was all the things David had accused him of and more. He lay in the sand, wrestling with idle thoughts of the harm he would inflict upon his captor if ever the situation allowed. He looked towards the horizon and imagined himself free of Bunce's tyranny; he pictured himself clawing at the beady eyes embedded in the man's simple, moon-shaped face.

There was a gentle thud behind him, as though something heavy had displaced the grey sand, and a boy's voice said: "You shouldn't be here. Pappy might find you. It isn't safe."

David spun round, the sound of another human voice—even one as timid as this—sounding utterly alien in the echoing sprawl of the Fade. A teenage boy, no more than sixteen years old, stood before him, smiling politely, legs together and arms clamped fiercely by his side. David wavered, not sure what he was staring at; the boy looked a little like a robot, he thought, or a malfunctioning machine.

He struggled to his knees and stared at the boy, who remained motionless, smiling down at him.

"I never heard you approaching," he said, which seemed to David the most disconcerting element of the boy's appearance. "Who are you?"

144

The boy remained perfectly still, as though he'd stood that way for a thousand years, having been painstakingly sculpted from a block of stone.

"I'm Philip," he said. He stared directly at the boy and smiled again. "I know who you are. You're the boy from the picture. The one I drew." He nodded, pleased with himself, as though he'd solved a difficult equation.

"I saw you," David said. "Over by the hills. You were being followed by a thin man. Then you both disappeared."

Philip's expression darkened and he glanced towards the unlimited horizon.

"Pappy doesn't like people being here. It's a secret place. Strangers don't belong."

"Is Pappy the thin man?" David said. "The one I saw following you?"

Philip nodded. His eyes shifted slightly to take in the hills and then settled once again on David.

"He knows you're here," he said. "He's like a wolf. He already has your scent."

David didn't like the sound of that one bit; he shifted his weight from his knees to his bottom and turned so that Philip could see his bound hands behind his back.

"I have to get out of here," he said. "Can you untie me?"

Philip stared at the twine wrapped around David's hands and considered the question for what seemed like an unfathomably long time. Eventually, he took a step towards David and knelt behind him. His delicate fingers began to work at the knots in the twine.

David felt a surge of relief; his chest swelled with so much hope he felt it as a physical pain across his rib cage. Tears threatened to spill down his cheeks, and he willed them away, remembering his rage at Bunce, and his growing fear of the oddly-shaped man with the vaguely unsettling name. He felt like he'd stumbled into a curious nightmare from which there could be no awakening; his imagination was tormenting him with images of the thin man stalking him across an empty landscape, and he attempted to dispel the fancy by engaging Philip as he worked at the twine.

"Are you a stranger here too?" he said, feeling the boy pick away at the knots.

From the corner of his eye he saw Philip pause for a moment. "I suppose I am, yes."

"So where did you come from?"

Philip looked up, surprised the boy had asked such an asinine question.

"Same place as you," he said, as though the answer was obvious. "Home."

He bent down and continued working on the twine binding David's hands. Whoever had secured the boy's wrists had made an impressive job of it. Philip's slender fingers couldn't find a single purchase of any note. He could feel the pressure in his knuckles as he strained at the combination of knots, but none of them would come loose. They defied every measure Philip attempted, no matter how concerted his efforts. He closed his eyes and tried again, sweat beginning to form along his brow. Still no joy; the knots were as obdurate as rock, a helix of stubborn ligatures fashioned solely to consign David to the Fade.

"It's no good," Philip said. "They're too tight."

David swiveled in the sand and felt every muscle in his body constrict. He could feel tears of rage welling in his eyes.

"*Fuck you, Bunce!*" he screamed. He tried to force his wrists apart until the violence of the gesture drew blood. "Please," he added, looking up at Philip and weeping freely. "You have to help me."

Philip had taken a precautionary step back and had assumed his odd robotic position in the sand.

"You're bleeding," he said. "And you have dried blood on your face. Pappy will smell you a mile away."

The observation was made with such cool detachment David ceased crying and glanced up, confused. Philip was staring at him as though at a captive animal, and David felt a sudden dizziness wash over him. Was that what he had become? The thin man's quarry, hamstrung and cornered, awaiting the final judgment of the knife? The notion terrified him, and he thrust his face into the dying light, urging Philip to relate to his pain.

"You can take me back," he said, sounding desperate and not caring in the slightest. "We can go home. You and me. Together."

Philip shook his head. "Only the person that brought you here can do that," he said. "You know the rules."

David stared at the strange boy and felt as though an active synapse in his brain had shut down.

"I don't know any rules," he said, trying to remain calm. "A man named Bunce tied me up and brought me here against my will. I don't even know what this place is. Do you understand? It makes no sense."

Philip frowned and tilted his head to one side. "Then why were you in my picture?"

David closed his eyes, fighting off a distant ache at the back of his skull.

"I don't know about any picture. I don't know anything about this place. I just want to go home. Please. You have to untie me. It'll give me half a chance when he comes back."

Philip raised his eyebrows. "Pappy?"

David shook his head. "The man who brought me here. I want to be ready when he comes looking for me again."

Philip stood before him, breathing steadily, displaying no visible emotion, and David wondered if he was a little dull in the head; it occurred to him that the boy had no sense of the severity of his situation. Perhaps Philip thought he was performing in a dream, one where nothing was ever expected to make sense.

He shook his head; he had no time to dwell on Philip's deficiencies. It wasn't a dream, not even close. He had the scars to prove it. The Fade, however improbable it might seem, was as real as sin. It was pointless debating otherwise. He was touching its dust, breathing its air; he could feel the sand in his throat and the wind whipping at the open wound in his brow. What greater proof did a man need? A black shape coalesced at the rim of his mind and a part of him insisted that everything he had ever done had brought him to the very edge of the Fade.

"Do you have a knife?" he said, dismissing the erratic nature of his thoughts and turning his attention back to Philip.

The other boy shook his head and then stopped as a thought passed almost visibly before his eyes.

"But I can get one," he said. "Wait here."

David opened his mouth, desperate not to lose his only ally, but in the space it took him to draw breath, the boy smiled, stepped forward, and flickered out of sight like a ghost.

Saul heard him before he caught sight of him, rifling through one of the drawers in his room. He frowned, trying to remember the last time Philip had willingly entered any bedroom other than his own. If there had ever been such an occasion, he couldn't recall it. He walked across the landing, pushed open the door, and stood watching his brother patiently sift through a cluttered drawer in his desk.

"Maybe I can help," he said. "What are you looking for?"

Philip barely looked up; he wiped a rogue strand of hair from his eyes and continued to comb through the drawer.

"Knife," he said quietly. "Cut free the hands."

Saul felt his blood run cold. He had heard Philip make similar grisly threats in the past; they all had. As a result, Mother had insisted that anything sharp be removed from Philip's reach, despite the inconvenience to the rest of the family. Every knife in the house was kept under lock and key. For everyone's safety, Mother said, though they all knew she really meant so that Philip didn't secretly cut himself in the night.

The only knife that fell outside this strict safety protocol was the one Saul had found down by the river. It was a steel grey Yato pocketknife, the kind used by anglers and campers; the blade was about four inches long and a little rusty. He'd hidden it away knowing full well that Mother would never allow him to keep it. How Philip came to know of its existence was anyone's guess. He had been guarded about handling it for fear of Father discovering his secret and thrashing him to within an inch of his life. He had hidden it away and all but forgotten about it; apparently Philip had not.

"You're looking in the wrong place," Saul said. "I'm not that stupid."

Philip stopped his search and looked across the room at his brother.

"It's important," he said. "I need it."

Saul entered the room and shook his head. "No knives. You know the rules."

Philip waited patiently, trying to see his way through to a rational explanation of why he required the knife, but all he could see was the comforting landscape of the Fade.

Saul walked across the room and closed the drawer before turning back to face his brother. "Why do you need it?"

Philip thought for a moment and then remembered. "I've found him," he said. "The boy in the drawing. He's all tied up."

Saul frowned, accustomed to following the tangled thread of

Philip's peculiar logic, but this one left him feeling hollow and confused.

"The boy in the picture isn't real, Philip. Neither's the Fade. It just seems that way because…" Saul faltered, uncertain how to end the sentence, before adding, "Because a part of you needs to escape."

Philip didn't consider arguing the point for an instant. He simply stared at Saul in that chilling, neutral manner of his, as though waiting for his brother to make the connection that would align their thoughts.

"Do you understand what I'm saying, Philip? It doesn't exist."

"I'll take you," he said. "You can see for yourself. You can help him."

Saul sighed, feeling a flare of exasperation. He readied himself to contradict his brother's position, but was stung by the memory of Philip striding across an open field, flickering like a character in a pre-war cartoon, wavering in and out of existence as though toying with Saul's limited perception. He had dismissed it as a visual anomaly, an aberration in the evening light. But what if he'd been wrong? What if the place in Philip's drawing was just a journey away, as easy to access as flipping open the page of a book? He pictured the boy in the image and remembered how lonely he had seemed; he had thought him a graphite representation of Philip, but perhaps he'd been wrong about that too. It briefly occurred to him that Philip had somehow managed to infect him with his craziness, had transmitted to him whatever impurity circulated in his blood, but his head felt clear, and when he held his hands up to his face his cheeks felt cool. It wasn't lunacy he was experiencing, it was altered perception. He was finally seeing the world through his brother's eyes.

"We don't have time for this," Philip said, surprising Saul with his clarity of purpose. "Get the knife."

Saul hesitated momentarily before he reached beneath his

mattress, dipped his hand into the torn fabric of the frame, and produced the Yato pocketknife. Philip nodded and moved towards him. He glanced quickly into Saul's eyes and then looked away. He clamped his arms around his brother's chest and whispered: "Don't worry, Saul. I won't let go."

Saul trembled at the contact, trying to remember the last time his brother had held him, as the wheel of reality turned.

Saul had inadvertently closed his eyes, not knowing what to expect, and when he opened them his first thought was: *I'm inside Philip's picture.*

He felt his brother release him and drew in a deep breath, marveling at the sense of dislocation he felt, trying to delve beyond what his eyes were seeing to isolate whatever axiom was holding this new land in place. There was a blue fringe of fluctuating light through which he could see a faint outline of his own bedroom; beyond that he could discern only the wind-whipped desert, the lowering sky and the dusty pelt of the hills. The lonely boy was nowhere to be seen.

Saul glanced to his left, sensing Philip's anxiety, and found him searching the horizon, his eyes darting between the black cracks in the earth.

"This place…" Saul said, still reeling from the sensation of having reality spun on its axis. "It really does exist."

Philip paid him no mind; he was too busy scanning the land for the boy.

"Where is he?" he said. "He should be here. I brought a knife, just like he asked." He turned to Saul and bore a look of utter despair. "I wanted to save him."

He waited, hoping for an explanation from his brother, but Saul was mesmerized by the dream-like element into which he'd been delivered. The two boys were momentarily lost to each other, each pursuing the answer to their own particular riddle; one hypnotized by beauty, the other overcome by grief.

"How is this possible?" Saul muttered, still reeling from the casual ease with which Philip had transported them. "It's all so…beautiful."

If he expected a response, he was left disappointed; Philip remained as far removed from Saul's incredulity, as Saul was from his brother's concern for the missing boy.

"You have to help me find him," Philip said, digging vainly with his hands in the dust. "I promised I'd come back." He looked up at Saul, who was still gazing at the last light bleeding across the sky. He reached up and grabbed at his brother's sleeve. "Saul. I need to find him. Why won't you help me?"

Saul shook his head as though dislodging a tenacious dream. He stared at Philip and was surprised to see how tired he looked. His face looked like it had just wrestled itself awake, and Saul could see every childhood loss Philip had ever experienced damming up behind his eyes. He stooped down and breathed slowly, considering his words carefully.

"You drew the boy in the picture, Philip. Remember? I don't think he was ever here. He can't have been. Look around; there's no sign of him. Or of anyone else, for that matter."

Saul waited while Philip cast another agonizing glance along the horizon.

"I think you're the boy in the picture," he added. "That might explain why you thought you were dying; because somehow you had the power to come here, to all this emptiness. This is what was hurting you, Philip. The Fade. This is what was making you ill."

Philip shook his head vigorously and emitted a muffled howl of frustration.

"I saw him. He was right here. His hands and feet had been tied. He could hardly move."

"Who brought him here?"

Philip rocked back and forth, agitated by his inability to produce the answers he knew his brother wanted to hear.

"I don't know." The distant roaring inside his head began to intensify, blocking out any hope of clarity in his thinking, and he clutched at the side of his skull.

"Was it you?" Saul said softly.

Philip shook his head. He hadn't brought the boy; someone else had. He knew that to be true. Even as his confidence began to waver, he knew he was not responsible for committing the boy to the Fade.

"But this is your secret place, Philip. If you didn't bring the boy here, then who did?"

Philip had no answer; his mind was growing dull and the noise inside his head was like a wind turbine running at full throttle. His frustration was almost palpable and he felt like weeping. The right answers eluded him, just as they always did. If they existed at all, they were like the answers to a theoretical formula: as remote and unreachable as the stars.

Philip stood up and looked across at the dark run of hills that swept along the desert floor. Something was tottering in and out of the shadows, hunched over like a man with a bad back, moving relentlessly among the scree, tall and alarmingly thin. Philip felt his breath falter in his throat; his bladder contracted and he was terrified that it would relax completely and embarrass him in front of Saul.

"There," he said, pointing towards a rocky outcrop into which the figure had disappeared. "Do you see?"

Saul strained his eyes and tried to suck the darkness from the hills.

"What am I looking for?"

"The thing with the sack," Philip said. "I saw it. You have to look hard. It knows where to hide."

Saul indulged him and let his eyes roam across the sterile land. He froze. Along the lower lip of the massed banks, a figure was deftly weaving between the crags. It moved like sludge, and was bent over like a coalman bearing an awkward load. Saul's hands grew clammy with sweat; his heart began to race. He was well acquainted with the subtle mischief of dread.

"Who is it?" he whispered, instinctively drawing his body closer to the ground so as not to be seen.

Philip paused for a moment, and then spoke with utter conviction. "It's Pappy," he said. "He must have taken the boy. I shouldn't have left him alone."

Saul glanced at his brother and saw a profound shame reflected in his eyes.

"This has nothing to do with you. Okay? Besides, I don't see any boy. Whoever's out there couldn't possibly have taken him. He's on his own."

A ghostly smile flitted across Philip's face.

"The boy's in the sack," he said. "That's what Pappy does. He cleans up the Fade. He puts them in his sack and he carries them to his house on the hill."

―――――――

By the time Bunce had dragged the tarpaulin halfway across the desert, the glamour of the Fade had been slowly ambushed by the dark. Pa led the way, stumbling occasionally in the rutted terrain, and Bunce followed, hauling Fliss's body with an equal measure of dismay and irritation. He tried to be as gentle as possible, easing her across the unforgiving desert, trying hard not to imagine what might be happening to the woman's face inside the tarpaulin as it bounced along the uneven ground. It made him feel sad. All of this had been Fliss's fault, he thought, but no one deserved to end their days like this.

Pa had come to terms with the situation quicker than Bunce had expected, but that was hardly much of a surprise. Pa was a survivor, and knew the value of adapting fast to any given situation. He always had. Bunce considered Ma's finger, lying buried in the woods, and realized this was not the first time his father had collaborated with the dark to conceal a crime. He felt a lump in his throat and Ma's face hovered in his mind's eye, smiling at him, her soft brown eyes as nurturing as freshly ploughed earth. He slowed down and lost his grip on the tarpaulin; he wanted to weep, not just for Ma, but for everyone his suffering had touched: the boy, Fliss, Gilly; even Pa, who continued to walk on, as silent and rugged as weathered stone.

Bunce drew to a stop and watched Pa take several vigorous strides into the dark, his large body slowly fading from view. He knew what he wanted to say, knew too that it would have to come out, but he felt hollow inside, as though finally articulating his anger would somehow drain him of every last drop of sorrow he had left. He drew in a breath and felt the wind dry out the walls of his mouth.

"I know about Ma," he said. "I've seen the box you keep in the woods, the one you keep visiting, sometimes in the middle of the night."

Up ahead, he sensed Pa stop; he slowly turned around to face him. He was still some distance away and Bunce could only make out the sharp angles of his father's face. He walked back towards his son until Bunce could see the simmering violence in his eyes.

"This is not the right time," Pa said softly. "We have business to attend to."

He turned away again, signaling the end of the conversation, but Bunce was far from finished, and he summoned the courage to probe deeper, to finally discover the truth about his Ma.

"I have a right to know," he said. Then, bracing himself for his father's reaction, added: "You killed her, didn't you? You and that bitch." He looked down at the tarpaulin and spat. "And now you can't live with the guilt."

Pa stopped and spun round, reeling as if from a blow; he held a hand to his brow and shook his head.

"Christ, Hilary. Is that what you think happened?"

Bunce swallowed, trying to solicit a clear moral conviction, and nodded.

Pa sank to his knees in the dust and Bunce thought he heard a single, wracking sob escape his lungs. His body was shaking, as though some hidden tumor was trying to erupt from his body, and his head was buried in his hands.

"You're right about the guilt, lad, that's for sure. But everything else..." Pa closed his eyes and lost himself in the despairing loop of the past. "I don't know. Perhaps I did kill her. I guess you'll have to decide that for yourself."

Bunce closed the gap between them and dropped to his knees. The wind capered between them; there was a thin veil of sand dancing before his eyes, distorting his father's face.

"What happened?"

Pa was unable to look him in the eye. Instead, he concentrated on the tarpaulin, hating its terrible freight, seeing the truth of his wife's departure in every dark crease, every pucker and groove of the oiled cloth. Bunce held his breath. He was close to finding out what had happened to Ma, and it all felt utterly surreal; the impulse to vomit in the sand was strong. When he gazed at Pa he looked like a broken man. Something deep inside had irrevocably shifted, and Bunce wondered what damage he might have caused by drawing him into the Fade and inviting him so close to the edge.

"Your Ma found out," Pa said. "About me and Fliss. That's the top and tail of it, lad." He lowered his eyes and Bunce realized he was remembering the very worst of himself. He was about to reveal the blackest part of his soul. "She caught us in the house and went berserk. Your Ma could be like that, Hilary. She had a hell of a temper on her when she was so inclined. Remember?"

Bunce nodded, recalling well enough Ma's outrage whenever he or Gilly neglected their chores.

"Fliss and I were in the kitchen," Pa went on. "We thought we had the house to ourselves, but your mother had other plans. She came in waving a meat cleaver and practically screamed the house down. She wasn't making any sense. Your mother and me, we'd been over for quite some time. We could barely stand to be in the same room. I think she suspected I'd been cheating for a while, lad, but when she found us in the house she went insane." He paused for a moment to let the sadness of that sink in. "She started waving the meat cleaver at us and vowed to kill Fliss where she stood. It seems impossible to imagine your Ma doing such a thing, I know, but she was a different person by this stage, Hilary. Not at all like the woman I once loved. She threw herself at Fliss and began swinging the knife, threatening to cut off her face. Then she changed tack and began threatening to injure herself unless I fucked Fliss on the kitchen floor. She said she wanted to witness my betrayal with her own eyes. I told her she was being irrational, that there was nothing going on between us and never had been, but your Ma wasn't stupid, and she howled even louder at my deceit. She placed her left finger on the surface of the kitchen counter and held the meat cleaver poised above it. I remember watching the gleam of the wedding ring in the fluorescent light. Your mother always joked it was the ninth circle of hell, and for all I know, she may have been right. She told me she would turn the ring into a symbol of my adultery unless Fliss and I started to undress. By this stage, she was almost psychotic. There was a wildness about her eyes that I'd never seen before. Fliss and I tried to calm her down, but it was in vain. All she could see was my black, worthless heart. When she chopped off that finger I don't think any of us expected quite so much blood."

Bunce gave a jolt, startled by the vividness of the image, feeling his mother's pain as a binding pressure stretching right across his chest. Pa stared at him for a moment, mildly concerned, before he lowered his eyes again and continued to rake through the ashes of his past.

"I thought that would be enough," he said, "but your Ma had other ideas. She lunged at Fliss with the meat cleaver, and Fliss knocked her down in self-defense. But she fell hard and cracked her head on the floor tiles. We were both expecting her to get up and come at us again, but she never moved. There was a lot of blood. All I really remember after that is the silence. The house suddenly seemed too small. I think I laughed because it seemed like something from a bad movie. It never occurred to me once, in all the time we stood listening to the silence, that your Ma might be dead. It was impossible, like trying to imagine the moon no longer orbiting the earth."

He sighed and allowed some of the dark sand to sift through his fingers, remembering the horror of the singular moment that had defined his life.

"I found the finger much later, when I was clearing up the mess. I couldn't bring myself to part with it. I placed it in your Ma's jewelry box and buried it in the woods. It felt like a sacrifice to lost love, the very last one your mother was prepared to make, but maybe I was wrong about that. I hated myself for doing it, but I had no choice. It was the only thing I could think to do to keep her near. The guilt of losing your Ma like that will never pass, Hilary, and a part of me never wants it to. Not really. The scars exist for a reason and each one ties me to the past. In a way, the shame I live with every day is your Ma's final gift to me. She never wanted me to forget what I did."

Bunce frowned, failing to understand some of the crude motives underpinning Pa's extraordinary tale.

"But you stayed with her," he said. "Fliss. You allowed her to move in to the house, invited her into the family. Why would you do such a thing?"

Pa smiled, but it was a weary, altogether comfortless gesture.

"Neither of us had a choice. It was a mess of our own making and we were in it together." He shook his head, bewildered now by the crazy logic that had governed them at the time, seeing it for the foolish covenant it had always been. "We were confused and afraid. Everything seemed distorted. It was hard to even think straight. We buried your Ma and left it at that. I asked Fliss to move in with us because I didn't trust her. How's that for irony?" He chuckled and followed my example by spitting in the direction of the tarpaulin. "I wanted her right under my nose where I could watch her every move. Funny, right?"

Bunce sat motionless, listening to the low whickering of the desert wind. He didn't think it was at all funny. He thought it was possibly the most wretched family history he had ever had the misfortune of hearing Pa disclose.

"So you didn't kill her," he said, tasting the bitterness of the statement but liking how it sounded all the same.

Pa spoke softly, a somber lament that could only just be heard above the wind: "Perhaps you heard a different story, lad, or maybe you weren't listening hard enough."

Bunce said nothing, unwilling to hear this theory elaborated upon, and Pa stood up.

"Grab the tarpaulin," he said. He turned and walked into the darkness of the Fade, a man with uncommon sorrow, grateful to have the silence returned.

The two brothers pursued the thin man across the unfamiliar darkness of the desert, never drawing too close to attract attention, but, at the same time, never straying too far behind.

Saul kept his eyes on the elusive figure as he dipped in and out of the crevices beneath the hills. He was moving at a steady pace, his long legs scissoring like a compass, his upper body stooped to accommodate the sack. Not for the first time Saul recoiled at the thought of what it might contain. He recalled Philip's slack face as he spoke the words that had filled him with dread. He remembered them now and wanted to run in the opposite direction, but the words themselves seemed to be drawing him on, urging him towards a revelation he felt ill-equipped to resist. He listened to them and felt the simple terror of their context: *He puts them in his sack and he carries them to his house on the hill.*

He glanced behind him and checked to make sure that Philip was still within touching distance.

"Are you sure he has the boy?" he whispered. Even as he spoke, Saul realized it was a telling question. There was no longer any uncertainty about the Fade, or even the thin man that Philip referred to as Pappy; circumstance and the testimony of his own eyes had confirmed both. All that remained was the distressing dilemma of what had become of the boy.

Philip nodded, wringing his hands, his face resolute.

"Is he still alive?"

Philip paused, reluctant to consider the question, but intuitively sensing its importance.

"I think so," he said, lowering his eyes. "But I'm not sure."

Saul could see how distressed Philip was, but disengaging at this point was not an option. If they were to help the boy they had to move fast; faster than Pappy, whose long legs seemed to be making light work of devouring the ground.

"This house he takes them to. Is it far?"

Philip shook his head again, more slowly this time.

"Do you know where it is?"

Philip stared at his brother. Saul could just make out the whites of his eyes. The fear Philip was feeling lay hidden in the black, dilated circle that was no longer visible to him, where the things Philip saw were rarely fully understood.

"It's in the hills," he said

Saul paused, suddenly curious. "Have you ever been inside?"

Philip shook his head and Saul realized he had been holding his breath, his relief when it finally came hitting him like an emotional flood. The force of it startled him and he looked up at the sky, astonished by the sudden brightness of the stars.

"If you've never been inside," he said, "how will you find it in the dark?"

Philip smiled and said, "Because I sometimes see it in my dreams." He looked thoughtfully at Saul for a moment, as though he were trying to piece together a random selection of clues, and then added: "Don't you?"

———

By the time they'd crossed the desert and reached the foot of the hills, their quarry had been claimed by the dark. Saul was once again beginning to question whether Pappy even existed; the notion of a thin, faceless man bundling children into a sack and taking them to a remote house on top of a hill sounded more and more like the fabric of one of Philip's recurring nightmares. He tried to visualize the figure as he walked, but realized that introducing any representation of the Pappy creature into his head would merely elicit night terrors of his own. Instead, he kept his head down, stayed within grabbing distance of Philip, and climbed the unsteady scree that lined the slopes.

After only a short time, Philip tapped him on the shoulder

and gestured for him to look into the sky. Saul glanced up and saw a ribbon of grey smoke snaking into the heavens. It was billowing from a chimney over the next rise, he thought, before its significance struck him like a blow. It was a signal, sent up by Pappy to ensure that he and Philip located the house. His blood ran cold and he clenched his fists until his nails bit into his skin. The bastard had sensed their presence all along. He had known they were following in his wake; had possibly even been expecting it. Saul cursed his foolishness. He stared at the grey smoke and watched it fade into an endless sky that his mind protested should never even exist.

"We should wait," he said, holding Philip back. "This doesn't feel right. I think he knows we're coming."

Philip smiled again. "Of course he does. Pappy knows every-thing." He made to set off over the hill towards the smoke, but Saul caught hold of his arm.

"What do you mean?"

"This is his creation. He knows every inch of it." He frowned and then broke into yet another smile as something dawned on him, something he'd never really appreciated before. "This place isn't the Fade," he said. "The house is."

Saul felt his heart begin to pound at the spinning abstraction Philip was attempting to articulate, just as his brother slipped free of his arm and accelerated into a run.

Saul chided himself for being so negligent and tore after him across the scree, but Philip had always been an easy runner and the gap between them widened with remarkable speed.

"Philip! Come back. It's not safe!" But he was out of earshot long before Saul's caution could find its mark, bounding effort-lessly over the rise towards the pillar of smoke.

Saul shook his head, almost weeping in frustration at Philip's recklessness, and ran across the hill in pursuit. When he reached the top he stopped, because Philip was standing waiting for him, breathing freely, staring across at a large grey house, perched at an odd angle atop an adjacent slope. Saul panted like a man who'd just labored over a marathon and gazed at the unusual structure on the hill. Light shone brightly from every window, as though it were eager not to be overlooked, and the chimney continued its ceaseless breathing into the sky.

Saul looked around, desperate to see other properties—a small village, perhaps—that might somehow diminish the compelling rarity of this one, but there was nothing other than rolling hills for miles around. The grey house was the only one of its kind, just as Pappy—its sole occupant, Saul guessed—was undeniably the only one of his.

He drew alongside his brother and they both stood in the darkness at the hill's crest staring at the illuminated house. Saul knew nothing about Georgian architecture, but he recognized the symmetry of the windows and the decorative pilasters either side of the door as a common enough feature in many newly-built homes. Where the grey house was unique was in the way it appeared to seamlessly merge with the ground on which it was built, as though it had sprouted from the compressed layers of muck beneath the hill.

"Impossible to miss," Saul said, staring at the lit windows.

"A light house," Philip said softly, and Saul nodded, surprised by his brother's insight. That was exactly what it was, he thought: a beacon, with the sole intention of seducing strangers with its false promise of warmth and hope.

"We should turn back," he said. "We have no reason to go in there. Not one."

"You're forgetting the boy."

Saul raised his hands to the sky. "We don't even know for sure if there is a boy. And even if there is, there's no guarantee he's in the house."

Philip stared at him and Saul was horrified to see that his

brother pitied him. He wanted to reach out and squeeze his throat until the very air around them, along with Pappy and the Fade, disappeared.

"He's in there," Philip said. "Pappy has him. He's waiting for us to try and take him back." He spoke slowly in the hope that Saul might finally understand.

Saul looked away, disgusted as much with himself as he was with Philip. The truth was, he didn't understand a single, depressing beat of what was taking place here, and never would. The Fade was like a dim recollection of a joke passed between friends; a grim narrative to invoke around a campfire; a fragile creature poised at the edge of its lair. Not only did Saul not understand it, he suspected it was unknowable, right to its very core, every last horrifying mote and morsel of it.

"You want to go in?" he asked.

"I don't have any choice."

Saul nodded, though it occurred to him later that maybe if he'd actually seen Pappy in the flesh, especially given Philip's chilling description of him, he might have been more insistent about turning back; but at this point a small part of him—the part that was clinging desperately to what he *did* understand, the floating memories of dead beer cans, warm rain, his cluttered room—was still inclined to humor his brother and treat this entire scenario as some kind of extended detachment disorder.

He took a tentative step forward, keeping his sights firmly fixed on the grey house, imagining a bald, mouthless, eyeless man, howling like the damned inside.

The tarpaulin containing Fliss's body was growing heavier by the second. Bunce could feel the muscles in his shoulders aching with the strain, and it was a great relief when Pa finally indicated a deep recess at the foot of one of the hills and said, "Let the bitch rot here, Hilary. It's as good a place as any."

Bunce dragged the tarpaulin into the recess and wedged it behind a rough belt of staggered rock. When he returned, sweating like a hog and dusting himself down, Pa was standing in the lee of the valley, staring up at the sky. He pointed.

"Smoke. From somewhere over the next hill, I reckon." He turned to look at Bunce, who could just distinguish Pa's lean outline. He looked like a figure separated from a paper chain, a lost spirit in search of soul mates, striking a lonely pose in the dark. "I thought you said no one else knew about this place."

Bunce felt a chastening heat in his cheeks and was glad that Pa couldn't see it. Though he'd told Pa that the Fade was his private kingdom, it would not be an exaggeration to suggest that he knew less about the place than he'd even dared to admit to himself. There were large parts of it that he'd never had the nerve to explore, the hills being a case in point. Their intimacy had always alarmed him; just thinking about trying to negotiate a way through the unstable scree made him feel claustrophobic. In truth, the Fade was as much a mystery to him as it was to Pa. If there *were* others, he'd certainly never seen them; but then, the Fade might not have wanted him to.

Pa stared at the sky for a moment, thinking. "Looks like chimney smoke," he said. "Maybe there's a house back there."

Bunce said nothing. He could feel himself hyperventilating; there was an almost palpable sense that he was losing control. The smoke rose in the sky like visual confirmation of a higher power at work in the Fade.

"Could be where that boy of yours is hiding," Pa said. He turned, waited for a reaction from his son and, when none was forthcoming, started walking up the slope of the hill.

Bunce stumbled after him. "Wait. We don't know what's up there. It could be anything."

"Could be," Pa said, and strode further into the starlit night.

Bunce cursed his dumb luck and ploughed after his father, neither as fleet of foot nor as intrepid as the man in front. He considered the smoke as he walked and what it might denote, but his thoughts always tended toward the bleak. Though he had visited the Fade on many occasions and felt blessed by its many freedoms, the place had always left a bitter taste in the mouth. He never felt as though the place had fully revealed itself to him and sensed now that there was a watching eye still to be disclosed. Scaling the rugged slopes in the middle of the night terrified him, not because he was unfamiliar with the terrain—though this was true—but because he knew that whatever sickness underpinned the place was almost sure to have its nest in the hills.

He pitched blindly after Pa, dislodging loose rubble and scree and, after what seemed like an age, finally joined him at the peak. His throat was on fire and his breathing was quick and erratic, but he felt a moment of sheer exuberance as he acknowledged the cold proximity of the stars. His eyes tracked across the heavens to the adjoining hill and he saw thick smoke billowing from the chimney of a large grey house. It was oddly positioned, as though a child had abandoned it in a fit of pique; lights were blazing in every window, illuminating the stone path to the door. There was something else, Bunce realized, something that seemed utterly out of place. He narrowed his eyes, recognizing the mundane nature of what he was seeing, but failing to appreciate the strangeness of seeing it here.

He blinked and looked again, but there was no denying its validity. Two boys were walking up the stone path towards the house, bathed in yellow light, one reaching out his hand, hesitantly opening the door.

10

AÜSLANDER

S aul opened the front door of the grey house and stepped inside. He was instantly overwhelmed; he held a hand up to his eyes and tried to blink away the dazzling light. He was struck by a wave of vertigo and felt nauseous, as though every perspective he had come to rely on had been flipped. It was like being bowled over by the sea and sucked down by the undertow. He reached behind him to check that Philip was still within reach and felt comforted when his brother's brittle fingers docked with his own.

His eyes began to adapt to the situation and he attempted to assimilate his new surroundings. The interior of the grey house was a monument to artificial light and appeared bigger within than without. This was because the ground floor was a single open-plan room of imposing proportions. Decorative parquet blocks lined the floor and dozens of modern spotlights embedded in the ceiling added dramatic illumination to the space. More startling still was that every available wall had been adorned with a display of floor-to-ceiling mirrors, their silver surface mesmerizing him with liquid light.

Saul felt his whole body tingling, as though he had walked into a pressurized room. When he looked around, countless Sauls stared back, glassy-eyed with fear; he could see the dazed expression on Philip's face endlessly repeating on itself, the terror of his dislocation reproduced as a single moment, captured again and again and again.

Saul tried to break the spell cast by the distorting effect of the mirrors, aware that there was still more to see. He braced himself and continued to absorb the skewed perspective offered by the grey house. Directly in front of him, some fifteen yards back, an elegant, freestanding staircase rose to the second floor, gold balustrades either side leading the way. Saul knew instinctively that the stairs were the toxic focal point of the structure; the banisters were like garish hooks luring him in, inviting him to run his hands along the gilt veneer and reach for whatever lay in the dim shadows above.

As if to confirm this, there was a subtle shift in the air at the top of the landing and a tall, thin figure appeared dressed in a grey suit. Everything about him looked wrong. A grey veil of skin was stretched across an overlarge skull, marbled with blue veins that looked like disconnected electrical wires; there was no face to speak of, just three simple black holes to signify eyes and mouth, as though his creator had started with the very best of intentions but neglected to finish the job.

Saul stared at Pappy for what seemed like an impossibly long time, hypnotized by his oblique configuration. Every aspect of his body appeared misshapen or exaggerated. His legs were absurdly long, elongated beyond the point of anything natural anatomy might permit, to the extent that Saul wondered if the thing were on stilts. They reminded him of the etiolated wooden pole his grandmother insisted on using to support the washing line in the back garden; or the grey, attenuated legs of a heron, balancing precariously in shallow water, patiently awaiting its prey.

Saul glanced down beside him and saw a yellow puddle spread around Philip's feet, his humiliation reflected half a hundred times around the room. There was no shame in that, he decided; his own bowels felt on the verge of loosening, and he squeezed Philip's hand hard in the vain hope that his brother might feel mildly reassured.

He looked up at the staircase again and saw what little darkness remained on the landing melt away. Pappy tottered out in full view, his grotesque appearance hideously defined; it occurred to Saul that whatever the thing was, wherever it came from, *this* was undoubtedly its home. As the shadows parted he noticed a large burlap sack at Pappy's feet, the kind farmers use to transport potatoes, and he felt a lancing pain across his chest. Whatever it was filled with wasn't resting comfortably in the sack. Crude lumps jutted out at odd angles and several dark stains measled the fabric, some still dripping through the cloth. He looked away, horrified by the detailed work his imagination was conducting on his behalf. He glanced across at Philip, praying that he hadn't noticed the burlap sack, but it was impossible to be certain; his expression had barely changed since he'd set foot in the door.

Saul closed his eyes for a moment, wishing himself away from the house and Pappy and everything this terrible place seemed to represent. He felt like his sanity was coming unstitched, that with each passing second in the grey house his control of the situation was diminishing. He opened his eyes and struggled to breathe, staring at Pappy, who was still wobbling uncertainly on his coarse, bird-like legs. He didn't know much, he decided, but he understood implicitly that, no matter what epiphany lay on the second floor of the house, he could not, under any circumstances, allow himself or his brother to be drawn there.

There was a noise behind him and he turned quickly, anticipating some kind of ambush. What he saw surprised him almost as much as seeing Pappy at the top of the stairs. Two men entered the house looking wary and defensive, one bald and fat with a peculiar moon-shaped face, the other weary and experienced, with a restless vigilance inhabiting the eyes.

Saul took a step to the side, pulling Philip with him, vaguely wondering how far his mind would stretch before it broke. The older of the two men, the one with the grizzled face and the searching eyes, took a moment to try and quantify the bizarre interior of the grey house and then fixed his gaze firmly on Saul.

"Where's the boy?" he said. His voice sounded soft, like a lullaby, completely at odds with the darting look that passed between him and his overweight companion.

Saul glanced towards the staircase, where Pappy was balanced on those long, ridiculous legs of his, the black holes of his eyes reflecting nothing but an ageless patience. He glanced again at the weeping sack at the thing's feet, feeling his stomach give an almighty heave, before he returned his gaze to the two men. They were both staring in synchronized horror at the faceless creature above the stairs.

"Holy God," he heard the older one mutter. "What am I seeing…?"

"My brother calls him Pappy," Saul whispered. And in so naming him, the teetering figure seemed released of whatever agent had been holding him back. He took one step forward, his ungainly legs chopping at the air, and began to slowly descend the stairs.

Saul glanced into the mirrored wall of the grey house and, for a short time, found himself drifting beyond Pappy and the Fade into a welcoming flatness that bore only a passing resemblance to reality. The Saul in the mirror was calm and reflective, blessed with the ability to assess everything with a cool, analytical eye.

His throat wasn't constricted with terror; his head wasn't pounding; his heart wasn't thundering in his chest. The Saul in the mirror was an observer, immune to the impulses that drive intellect and blood, perfectly safe behind the undulating liquid light.

Saul smiled and the Saul in the mirror smiled too; when he looked back at the stairs, Pappy had already negotiated half of them, and instantly the illusion of the mirrored world was gone. His throat felt like sandpaper; his head throbbed, anchoring him to the spot; his heart roared like a caged animal. What little control he still had of his body's physical response to Pappy's descent was required to prevent him vomiting in fear.

He risked a look to his left and realized that Philip had barely moved since he'd arrived; he was as compelled by the strange spectacle of Pappy's child-like movement on the stairs as the two men who stood watching by his side.

Saul shook his head, trying to dislodge whatever influence seemed to be clogging up his mind, but the atmosphere in the room had grown ponderous and still, and all he could do was behold Pappy's final doddering steps as he claimed his place at the foot of the stairs. Saul glanced behind him and saw that the front door was still wide open; it was no more than half a dozen steps away, but it could easily have been a thousand for all the conviction he felt that he might be successful in bridging the gap. Pappy, or the grey house, or possibly even the Fade, was inside his head. Now that it had taken root, Saul imagined that it would squat there for eternity, or until Pappy had done to him what he had done to the boy. He remembered Philip telling him that Pappy's job was to clean up the Fade, and here they all were, boxed inside the grey house, their horror reflected back at them, as the place's caretaker attended to his work.

He noticed that there were now too many Pappys to count, the mirrors multiplying his ghoulish physique. He was much taller than even Saul imagined, and, despite himself, he found himself admiring the thing's intricate composition, no matter that he was an affront to a host of natural laws. It occurred to Saul that everything the Fade represented—lost hope, unfulfilled promises, ill-fated deliverance—was encoded in the genes of the thing it had created to protect it. Pappy was what happened to freedom when it was denied; faith when it was aborted; love when it was inevitably lost. Saul knew this because the thing inside his head told him so; the realization felt raw, like having a harrowing premonition confirmed.

He stared at the grey-veiled skin pulled taut over Pappy's face and was unsurprised when the smooth surface finally began to shift. He watched, fascinated by this new development, and lost himself in the rhythmic rippling of the skin. Eventually, a face began to take shape, and Saul trembled as the familiar features locked onto his own…

***

Saul gazed upon the face of his father and, feeling a sudden burden of responsibility, spoke:

–You shouldn't be here. It's dangerous. You might get hurt.

–Then why are you here?

–I came to help Philip. He needed me. I couldn't let him come here alone, could I?

–You were always a good kid, Saul. Looking out for Philip and Amy. Put me to shame, really.

[Pause]

–That's not true.

–We both know it is, son. Deep down. But that's okay.

–It's been hard for all of us. Philip's…

–I know. 'Special', right?

[Laughs]

–He's different. Sees things none of the rest of us can. Not even Mother.

[Pause]

–A saint, your mother. I wonder how she feels being married to a drunk?

–What's it like being married to a saint?

[Laughs]

–Imagine that. The drunk and the saint. A marriage made in hell.

[Pause]

–Why do you do it?

–Do what?

–The drinking.

[Pause]

–It's complicated, Saul. I don't have an easy answer.

–Does it take away the pain?

[Pause]

–No. Not really.

–So why do it?

–That's not the correct question, Saul. The really relevant question always seems to be 'why not'?

–It hurts everyone. The whole family.

–I know.

[Pause]

–Don't you care?

–More than you can possibly imagine.

[Pause]

–I've never heard you say I love you, Father. Not once. Not even to Mother.

[Pause]

–Would it have made a difference?

–I don't know. It just seems strange. I've heard you say you love beer; I've even heard you say you love the horses…

–That's different and you know it. It's meaningless.

–Then what do you really love?

[Pause]

–I love that your favorite shirt is the black one with the melting Rubik's cube on it; I love that Philip touches his nose when he's about to sneeze; I love that Amy squeals like a dolphin when she's playing in the bath; and I love that your mother always falls asleep whenever she picks up a book.

[Pause]

–I want to cry but I don't think I can. I'm too scared.

[Pause]

–Remember that feeling, Saul. When it becomes impossible to think about anything else, you'll know you've been condemned to suffer the same fate as your old man.

Pa rubbed his face, unable to believe what was happening before his eyes. The thing at the bottom of the stairs was transforming, the skin wrapped over its molded skull rippling, changing, coveting a more human shape, the black holes of the eyes and mouth reconfiguring to form a face that was wholly recognizable, though it had been a while since he had seen it in the flesh...

Pa gazed upon the face of his deceased wife and, losing himself to the memory of what they had once shared, spoke:

–Esther. I'd forgotten how beautiful you are.

–I doubt that it matters now, William. Too much water has travelled under the bridge, don't you think?

–I suppose so, yes.

–How have you been? *[Pause]* Bill? Are you okay?

–I'm not sure. It's such an odd question…so damn *normal.*

–What would you prefer?

–I want you to howl in frustration at what happened, scream down the heavens until you're blue in the face!

[Pause]

–I already tried that, remember?

–But things are different now.

[Pause]

–Not much has changed. Not really. We're both still pretty much the same.

–God, Esther! What a fool I've been. What happened to us; what in God's name went wrong?

–Life just got in the way, Bill. It has a habit of doing that sometimes. If you take your eye off the ball for a second, you can lose everything.

[Pause]

–The day it happened. You were so crazy. You had a meat cleaver, for Christ's sake…

–None of us can be proud of anything that happened on that day, Bill. Blood had to be spilled; it's just a shame it ended up being mine.

–I think about it every day. It used to make me angry. Now the guilt just gnaws away at me, eating me up from inside…

[Pause]

–It'll pass soon enough, I'm sure.

[Pause]

–I screwed up the kids, Esther. They grew up so fast. I don't know who they are anymore.

–I'm not sure you ever did, Bill. You were always too busy.

–There was a lot to do.

–I know. Yet somehow you always found time for her…

[Pause]

–I got rid of her. She betrayed me. She seduced Gilly…

[Pause]

–Then you finally understand the pain of having your heart ripped open by someone you thought you could trust...

–The kids. They miss you like hell.

–They'll recover, in time.

–I miss you too.

–I know you do.

[Pause]

–Is it too late to beg your forgiveness?

[Pause]

–Fall to your knees and beg away, Bill, and let's see if forgiveness can be bought so cheaply. I guess only the gods know the answer to that.

–Then I'll ask them every night, before I sleep.

[Pause]

–When you find the right prayer, let me know...

Hilary Bunce was shaking inside. His eyes were wide, his mouth hung open revealing a crooked dental disaster, and the noises in his head were throttling any attempt to rationalize what he was witnessing. The thing at the bottom of the stairs—a little like a scarecrow, he thought; a little like a Hallowe'en monster—was somehow reconstructing the limited features of its face. He watched on, unable to look away, as the silver veil of skin clinging to the creature's skull rippled and swam before his eyes, a glistening enchantment, coaxing out the awful details of a face he would never be able to forget...

Hilary Bunce gazed upon the face of Fliss and, struggling to articulate his conflicted emotions, finally spoke:

–I don't like this. I want you to leave.

–That's not going to happen, honey. We have unfinished business. Who were you expecting? Your Ma? That boy you abandoned in the Fade?

–I wasn't expecting anyone.

–Maybe that's why I'm here. To fill the void. To show you the value of being prepared for the worst.

–I know why you're here. You want to try and make me feel bad about myself, just like you did when you were alive.

–You did that to yourself, cowboy. You were your own worst enemy. Look closely and see for yourself...

Fliss's features morph into a mask of Bunce's moronic, moon-shaped face and he briefly stares into his own troubled eyes, before the charm evaporates and Fliss's hateful glare realigns itself on the creature's skull...

–Tell me what you just saw.

–I don't want to.

–That's because you saw what everybody else sees when they look at you, Hilary. A gutless, inflatable balloon.

[Pause]

–I'm not those things. I never have been. If I were, maybe you'd still be alive.

–*[Laughs]* The one time you found a little spunk in that shriveled ball sack of yours. Good for you, soldier.

[Pause]

–Don't call me that!

–What? Soldier?

[Pause]

–I don't like it.

–Ah! The simple psychology of the fractured family unit. It reminds you of Gilly, doesn't it?

[Silence]

–He has the spirit of a marine, a real man of action; I always liked that about him. *[Pause]* He was the one you looked up to, wasn't he? The one you always admired, even when you were young boys... *[Pause]* Would you like me to tell you about his cock? Is that it? What it felt like compared to your Pa's? *[Chuckles]*

–You're disgusting. You always were. I don't know what Pa or Gilly ever saw in you. You make me feel sick.

[Pause]

–Are you sure, Hilary? I don't think that's quite true, do you? Maybe you feel something else, something that you don't quite understand, something that makes you feel hot and lonely and angry and confused...

–Shut up! Just shut up! Pa was right, you're a sick bitch who deserved to die. I'm glad I fucking killed you!

–You wondered what it might be like, didn't you, Hilary? Even before you found out about me and Gilly. You'd lie awake at night with your best intention in hand and imagine what it might be like if you could just spend a single hour alone with the whore in your father's bed...

–*Stop it!* Please. I never did anything like that. Not once.

–...and when you finally did find out about me and Gilly, your curiosity grew, didn't it? If I'd been with two, you wondered, why not three? Is that how it was, Hilary? Is that the sickness you've been hiding from yourself all these months? Is that the guilt that's slowly been rotting away your feeble brain?

–*[Softly]* You're not real. None of this is real. I don't have to listen anymore...

–You betrayed him, Hilary. Just as much as Gilly. Nothing you can say or do will ever change that; not now, not ever. It will haunt you to the end of your days.

–*Please!* Haven't you done enough damage? Leave us alone!

–Remember, Hilary: every time you close your eyes, I'll be waiting...

Philip's face was pale, his skin felt feverish, his eyelids seemed to be scraping fresh trauma across his vision every time he blinked. Pappy was standing at the bottom of the stairs, watching him, his long pianist's fingers stirring, reminding Philip of a spider's brittle legs dancing across the surface of its web. He tried to avert his gaze, but the slow movement of the fingers tapping against Pappy's leg was mesmerizing, like watching the compelling, yet ultimately fruitless, endeavor of the gudgeon he had kept in the jar. When he was finally able to pull his eyes away, he noticed that Saul and the two strange men were also watching Pappy closely, as though they could see something far more diverting than the black holes rippling and spreading across its crude excuse of a face. He stared again at the graceless figure and wondered what had happened to the uncomplicated beauty of the Fade. Pappy's face wanted to tell him; it stretched and contorted, bleeding shades of darkness and light across the yielding skin, until it finally acquired the familiar features of a young boy, bloodied, lost and alone...

Philip gazed upon the face of David and, delighted to have finally found him, spoke:

–You're the boy! The one I was trying to help. *[Pause]* What happened to you?

–That doesn't matter right now. The point is you found me. You've come a long way. I didn't think I'd see you again.

–I brought a knife. Just like I said.

–Can I see it?

–My brother has it. He looks after things like that. It's very sharp.

–You did a good job, Philip. I always knew you'd find your way back.

[Pause]

–I don't like this house. There are too many mirrors. You can't see what's out there, only what's trapped inside.

–*[Smiles]* I'd never thought of it like that.

–I don't like Pappy either. His face is like Father's when he's angry—black eyes staring, black mouth like a tunnel, shouting. He makes me scared.

–That's okay, Philip. He makes me scared, too.

[Pause]

–Saul says it's important to face your fears. He tells me not to be afraid of being afraid. *[Laughs]*

–What are you most afraid of?

[Pause]

–Dying.

[Pause]

–There are worse things than dying…

–Maybe so, but I can't imagine them.

–Good. *[Smiles]* Imagination's overrated.

[Pause]

–Can I go home now? I'm getting tired.

–I don't think so, Philip. The door's closing. When it finally shuts, you'll be here for a long time, just like me…

–But I can't. Saul and I have to get back.

–It's too late, Philip. It's already begun. But that's okay. We can talk like this forever. We can keep each other company in the grey house… You and I and Saul, and Pappy… Talking until it's time to fade…

Philip wrenched himself from the trance and saw the ghost of David's smile slip in the distorted ruin of Pappy's face. The features converged like meat in a blender, leaving behind a pulped compound of bright-eyed adolescence and eternal darkness, the two spliced together in a meaningless frenzy of facial tics, the best and worst of Pappy and David combined.

He stared into the shifting, unknowable face and released an endless scream, long and loud, until his lungs hurt, not knowing what it was that he was screaming, just acutely aware that he had to shatter the terrible silence and break the hold that Pappy seemed to have on every unfortunate captive in the room. The mirrors on the wall were showing a portrait of some unfathomable perversion taking place, Pappy's face continuing to writhe with the spirit of both the lost boy and the lost soul, each vying for dominion of the protean flesh.

He glanced behind him and saw that the door of the grey house was slowly closing, and when he turned back, the battle raging in Pappy's face had been won. The startled features of David—still unsettled and seeming to crumple like dried wax in the flux—stared at him for a moment, before staring past him in panic at the door.

"*Run!*" he screamed. "Quickly, Philip. You have to leave. Run now, as fast as you can. *Ruuuunnn!*"

As the last syllable fell from David's mouth there was a sustained roar of disapproval and the black eyes and mouth of Pappy's face fell like a dark scourge across the buckling skin. The skull atop the creature's tottering frame was one vast black hole, into which all manner of disgraces had been poured. Pappy reached out a flailing hand, sensing the emptiness of his failure, and unleashed a desperate, uncontrollable lament.

Philip—mobilized by David's frantic counsel—heard only a

fraction of Pappy's cry as he shoved Saul unceremoniously towards the door. It was closing fast, but there was still room, still enough space to squeeze two terrified boys, grown intimate with the caprices of the Fade, into the arms of their own slumbering, dispassionate world.

Unhesitatingly, Philip wrapped his arms around his younger brother and launched them both towards the narrowing door. They spilled out of the grey house and tumbled onto the stone path, just as the heavy door slammed shut behind them. Philip glanced down at Saul, breathing hard. He had hurt his side when he landed, and his head still felt fuzzy from listening to David's voice. He stared at Saul again and then they both looked towards the grey house. The door was firmly closed, but in the blinding light beyond the windows, they could see Pappy's shadow moving inexorably towards the two men.

Still holding on to his brother for dear life, Saul said: "Quickly. We don't have much time. We need to get home."

Philip nodded and tightened his grip around Saul's chest; he closed his eyes and felt a band of pressure in his skull as he tried to find his way back, the coolness of the night chilling the film of sweat that was prickling his brow. The customary sensation of accelerated flight combined with sublime wonder failed to materialize. All Philip felt was a mounting sense of dread; other than that: nothing.

"What's the matter?" Saul said, his whole body straining with anticipation.

Philip stared into his brother's eyes; they were so close, their skulls were almost touching.

"It doesn't want to take me," he said. "It feels different."

Saul clenched his fists and made an effort to stay calm. "Try again. Maybe you're too tense. I know it's hard, Philip, but you have to relax a little. Okay? Just take a deep breath and take us home."

Philip closed his eyes and braced himself for the coiled flux of departure; he squeezed his eyes together so hard he saw yellow stars pin-wheeling like moths behind his lids. When he opened them again, his face crumpled and tears of frustration flowed down his cheeks. There had been no change; he was still outside the grey house, holding onto his brother for dear life. It was as though the bright light—into which he usually effortlessly slipped —had gone dark.

"It's Pappy," he said, fighting back the tears. "He doesn't want us to leave. He's too strong."

Saul drew back, pulling his body away from his brother and breathing heavily into Philip's restless face.

"We haven't time for this shit," he said. "We have to get home. Please, Philip, try and relax. The reason it's not working is because you're too agitated. It has to be."

Even as Saul was speaking, he realized his tone was counter-productive, the entreaty only likely to increase his brother's anxiety rather than relieve it. Saul needed to transmit patience, not discomfort; Philip represented their only chance of extricating themselves from whatever hellhole they had stumbled into. He had brought them here, and he was the only one who had the capacity to guide them out.

He glanced back towards the house, hoping to see Pappy illuminated in the window, still preoccupied with the two men. He frowned, craning his head for a better view. The window showed nothing but reflected light. Instinctively, Saul turned his head and scanned the dark hills, half-expecting to see the long legs of Pappy powering towards him, that dreadful sack thrown over his shoulder, the rustle of the burlap drilling into his brain like an echo of some grand atrocity, the sealed contents bleeding into the churned earth of the Fade.

He thought for a moment that he might be sick and sucked air into his lungs as he returned his gaze to the house.

"You want me to keep trying?" Philip said, looking utterly dejected, as though the failure to leave was a by-product of his own deficiencies.

Saul felt like weeping then and almost succumbed, only the terror of the moment holding it in abeyance. He could feel his brother's heat, the fiery life of him pressed against his body, their heartbeats so close they could practically be beating as one.

"You're doing great, Philip. Just hold on tight and keep going. You're almost there."

This was a skill Saul had learnt from their mother, and he was rather surprised to discover that, as the crisis deepened, his response to it became increasingly controlled.

He risked another glance at the house and felt a sudden tightening in his chest. The door of the grey house, through which only moments ago they had passed to relative safety, was being eased open with exquisite slowness from the inside.

He disentangled himself from Philip's warm embrace and, as calmly as he could, said: "Okay, Philip, time's up. We'll try again later. Right now, we need to move. You think you can manage that?"

Philip looked confused. "Where will we go?"

Saul watched the door—found himself unable to take his eyes off the creeping horror of it—and said, "We'll go back down the hill. Away from the house. You might be okay down there. There'll be no…interference."

Philip paused for a moment, processing Saul's logic, and then nodded in agreement, a sadness lodged deep within his eyes.

The door inched open, as though wedged in treacle, and Saul glimpsed a long, thin leg insinuate itself into the darkness. Behind it, unfolding like an eel, seeped the body and expressionless face of Pappy, advancing like a black glacier, re-joining the night with a cool, relentless purpose.

Saul's skin grew cold and his fingers felt suddenly numb. "I need you to stay focused," he said. "Keep your eyes on the ground and watch where you're walking. Don't go too fast and don't look back."

He knew that Philip's instinct would be to glance over his shoulder to see what was going on, but he took his brother's chin in his hand and grimly held on, forcing him to stare into Saul's eyes.

"Forget the house. It's a bad place, Philip. We need to get as far away from it as possible, as quickly as we can. Okay?"

Philip nodded and allowed himself to be led back down the stone path. Saul turned his head and risked another quick look at the opening door and this time Pappy had fully emerged from the house. He looked stitched together from the lowest point of humanity's evolutionary line, transporting in the flat smear of his face a great sorrow that pooled in the black holes of his eyes. As Saul watched, Pappy caught him in his gaze and the whole of his face lit up like a headlamp, casting yellow illumination across the hillside, the gathered darkness quick to submit to the light. Saul drew in a startled breath. The simple dark holes in Pappy's face were now burning with orange fire and the effect—more like a dream of light than light itself—spilled across the broken scree of the hill. Pappy seemed to hesitate for a moment, acclimatizing to his new perspective, before he began loping towards them down the path.

Saul paled as he felt the cold wash of Pappy's dreamlight strike his face; he grabbed Philip by the arm, muttered a short, breathless prayer, and launched himself down the side of the hill.

"Stay close!" he yelled. "When we reach the bottom, head for the shore."

Their progress down the slope was a barely-controlled tumble, the two of them stumbling and slipping on the uncertain terrain. Behind them, Saul could hear Pappy executing an implacable course down the same slope, the dreamlight blazing across the hill, searching out the fugitives with uncompromising accuracy, no matter how often Saul deviated from their original track.

As they ran—Saul clinging to Philip with a kind of paternal fury, his blood thundering through his veins—he tried to imagine how many others had visited this place, only to be scooped up by the creature in the grey house and sealed inside its sack, lost forever in a world that should never exist. The idea was too big, too illogical to consider for long, and he felt his head pounding with a hollow, disconnected hysteria as his feet crunched over shifting gravel and scree.

In no time at all, they reached the bottom of the hill and Saul dragged Philip into the open desert, the deep blackness as dense as tar.

Philip moaned and, without looking over his shoulder, said, "He's coming. I can feel him. It's pointless trying to run. This is his home."

Saul turned on him and grabbed him by the throat. "Bullshit! We keep running. We stay calm, and we run until we drop. Just keep trying to get us out of here. I'll figure out the rest."

They set off again into the vastness of the desert, Pappy's dreamlight flickering across the sand behind them, their bodies already tiring as they headed for the distant shore up ahead. There was a heaviness in Saul's limbs that made him feel like an old man and he cursed his weak body, aware that he had only a short distance left in the tank. If Philip wasn't able to flick the switch that hoisted them out of here, their journey's end would rear up before them in a flash of unnatural light. Saul imagined Pappy's tapered fingers reaching for them as they fell, tearing into Philip's tender flesh and shoving great hunks of it into the brimming sack. It was no longer enough to vow that he wouldn't allow such a thing to happen; the prospect was upon them, the reality too close to ignore. Pappy was no more than a heartbeat behind and Saul had no idea how to elude him; only knew now—the realization hitting him with the intensity of a migraine—that the creature could not be out-run.

Another quick glance over his shoulder and this time Saul slowed down, uncertain of what was happening. Pappy's rhythmic pursuit appeared to have stalled; rather than continuing to follow them across the desert, the creature was poised about fifty yards away, utterly motionless, standing like a scarecrow in the middle of a field. His long arms were stretched out either side of him and his fragile, pianist's fingers were gyrating slowly, moving the air around him in expansive circles, agitating the desert sand below; worse still, wedged against Pappy's stalk-like legs, in the disturbance of earth and grit, Saul could just discern the bulging menace of the sack.

Saul stood for a moment, hypnotized by the peculiar sight, half-aware even as his body defied him that they were losing valuable time. The dreamlight emanating from Pappy's face intensified and bathed both Saul and Philip in a deluge of blinding light.

Briefly unsighted, Saul felt slivers of the dreamlight pierce his retinas, showing him lost footage of whatever sickness nestled inside the creature's head. He caught blurred images of flyblown meat, weeping children, holocaust labor camps and the shredded rags of aborted life. The revelation was only fleeting, but it was enough. Saul sank to his knees, held captive by Pappy's dreamlight, and knew instantly that the appalling vision had completely drained him of hope.

When he opened his eyes, he realized that the dreamlight was dimming and that Philip too had fallen to his knees. He looked close to tears and Saul felt a sudden rush of affection for him, a flutter of unadulterated love that made his heart ache beyond measure.

He looked across at Pappy and was unsurprised to see that the gyrating fingers animating the desert sand had evolved into something far more dramatic. Pappy was now moving his arms in slow, deliberate circles, his limbs wheeling through the air and generating a vast pressure that was stirring the sand into a tumultuous cyclone of whirling dust, through which it was becoming increasingly difficult to see. Pappy was still visible, as was the strange dreamlight pouring from his face, but staring into the rapidly escalating windstorm was like trying to penetrate a thick mist.

Saul rose to his feet and attempted to push his way through the squall of sand, but was thwarted by the intensity of it. Philip, too, was on his feet, looking dazed and lost, seduced by a simple glamour that he hadn't the wit or inclination to resist.

"*Philip!*" Saul screamed. "*Get over here!*" But if his brother heard him, he showed no sign of it. If anything, he seemed to be moving inexorably closer to Pappy, who stood motionless now in the centre of the storm; the dreamlight was blazing again, and Philip appeared to be the focal point of the creature's calculated regard.

Saul pushed against the spinning grains of sand in front of him, cursing the element's defiance of him, and screamed his brother's name into the rising wind. It was no use; Philip was treading a different path and, in small increments, the storm was ushering him directly into Pappy's open arms.

Saul sank to his knees again and beat the ground with his fists. Whatever this place was, with its rolling hills and grey house and appalling custodian, it was evident that it could not be defeated; not even by a furious kind of brotherly love.

Saul lifted his head and gazed at the creature manipulating the sand. The dreamlight in his face had dimmed again and Saul watched on in horror as Pappy contorted the black hole of his mouth in an attempt to shape and articulate its pain. A sound emerged, raw and gravelly, as though forged in the belly of the storm raging around them; and then, shockingly, a single word, audible even above the wind and despite the rasping cadence of the voice:

"*Stand.*"

Saul looked across at Philip, trying to gauge the distance between them, and then rose to his feet.

"Please!" he shouted, desperate to be heard above the storm. He was struggling to find the right words, uncertain whether to kneel in obeisance or scream defiantly into the creature's face; he vaguely wondered how many words he would be allowed to utter before his heart was ripped from his chest. "We can work this out," he continued. "You don't have to do this."

Pappy seemed to listen for a moment, teetering on his delicate legs, before offering a labored, guttural reply.

"*I must.*"

Saul shook his head and fought to take a step forward, concerned not with communication but with carving a path through the storm towards his brother.

"You can stop. You can let us go."

The black hole of Pappy's mouth fluttered, simulating speech. "*There is no let go. Only this.*"

He pointed to the sack by his side and Saul felt his bowels loosen and the lining of his stomach start to cramp. In the Fade, Pappy's sack was the last act of some defining nightmare, where the trail of the imagination—*any* imagination—had to stop.

Frantically, Saul said: "But we don't belong here!"

The storm raged around them and Pappy shook his head. "*You are wrong. You were curious and eventually you found what you were looking for. You found me.*"

"We're just children," Saul said, inching closer to Philip across the shifting sand. "We shouldn't even be here."

"*Yet here you are. Lost children. Looking for a safe place. A happy place. Away from everything.*"

Saul glanced to the left and saw that Philip was being drawn towards Pappy's dreamlight again, the mesmerizing glow luring him ever closer to the bright edge of whatever destiny lay concealed in the sack. Saul pushed against the storm, desperate to reach him, but was violently repelled and landed flat on his back in the sand. He felt something dig into the waistband of his jeans and pretended to roll over in pain, remembering the knife, the one Philip had asked him to bring along to rescue the boy. He gasped for breath, pulled the Yato pocketknife from his jeans, and wrapped his palm around it, taking comfort and hope from the sudden heft of it in his hand. Its blade might be a little dull, Saul thought, but it was better than nothing; even a dull blade could rip open what passed for eyes in a counterfeit face.

He stood up and faced Pappy again, shielding the hand containing the knife, thinking fast, looking for a way to occupy the creature's attention.

"We made a mistake" he said. "That's all. A *mistake!*"

"*You made a* choice," Pappy said. "*And now here we are. In the happy place. With dust in our hair and blood on our hands. Waiting for the end to come, as it must.*"

It was almost as though the creature were offering Saul a cue. He unfolded the blade of the Yato pocketknife from its case, lowered his head, and ploughed forward into the storm. He pictured Philip, suspended in the headlamp glow of the creature's face, terrified beyond belief and failing to understand a single second of what was happening to him; he then thought of Father lying on the floor of the kitchen back home in a pool of his own blood, put down by Saul himself in a fit of rage, unable to reconcile the difference in that moment between what had been lost and what, in the final reckoning, might be gained. Then came Mother, a force of nature whose spirit would not be broken, not even by her crazy family, who had so many flaws it was hard to see where the good stuff began. And finally, pushing Saul beyond the influence of the Fade, with its crushing storm and powerful custodian, levering him onto a plane that felt almost mystical: the simple, smiling face of Amy, his sister; the girl who planted flowers and collected leaves and buried fledglings that had fallen from their nest; the girl who followed Philip unconditionally and without reason, merely because she wanted to be close; the girl who he wanted to see again, playing in the garden, doing normal things in a normal world on a normal day.

He bellowed with all the fury of a broken man, buffeted his way through the storm and took a running leap at his target, easily knocking Pappy to the ground. The attack seemed to come as a surprise, and Pappy offered no resistance short of a flailing arm, his doddering legs folding underneath him, sending even more dust and debris into the air.

The face, Saul thought. *Go for the face.* He gritted his teeth and felt the heat of some primal energy coursing through his body. He was operating purely on instinct now, responding to the only impulse that mattered: fear. He raised his left hand, unleashed one more tribal shriek, and plunged the blade of the Yato pocketknife deep into Pappy's face. The storm ceased instantly and the dreamlight began to fade, as though it were on a dimmer switch, discharging instead an endless torrent of darkness. Saul, barely visible to Philip anymore, pulled back his arm and lunged again, this time tearing into one of the black holes of the creature's eyes; his hand went numb, as though it had been dipped in a bucket of ice, and he had the disconcerting sensation that the black hole was bottomless, his hand reaching down into a space that stretched into a cold, loveless infinity.

"Philip!" he shouted, looking over his shoulder into the darkness. "Are you okay?"

There was a momentary silence; Saul waited.

"It's gone dark," his brother said. "I don't know where I am."

Saul laughed then, a wild, hysterical, loon-like wail that floated out across the desert and reverberated in the nearby hills. Without pausing to think about what he was doing, or what it might mean, Saul blinked away tears and tore madly at the remainder of Pappy's face with the blade until the grey skin stretched across the skull was nothing more than ragged strips of flayed flesh, betraying the imperfect limits of the creature charged with preserving the Fade.

When he was finished, Saul climbed off Pappy's lifeless body, threw the knife into the darkness of the desert, and found his way back to his brother.

"Is it gone?" Philip said, allowing himself to be hugged.

Saul closed his eyes, searching for the right answer. "Forever," he said, squeezing hard, hearing his own lie and wanting to believe it. "You think you'll be able to take us home now?"

He felt Philip shrug and then wrap his arms around Saul's body. Saul closed his eyes, held his breath, and prayed. Almost immediately, there was a delicate shimmer in the atmosphere, a rush of light, and a trembling obligation between Philip and whatever power he possessed.

When he next breathed out, it was raining and he could see their house in the distance, about half a mile away. He looked at Philip, smiled, dusted himself down, and the two of them began to walk across the grass. Philip stuck out his tongue and turned his face to the heavens and Saul, feeling a child-like freedom, did the same. The sky looked enormous, without end; the rain had never tasted so sweet.

EPILOGUE

The house sounded quiet. A little too quiet, and Saul led Philip through the kitchen and into the living room, where they found Amy sitting on the floor with a picture frame and a bowl of dried flowers. Mother and Father were sitting in their recliners watching a game show. Father chuckled occasionally when a contestant stammered a ludicrously incorrect answer, and Mother tutted at his misplaced amusement, before smiling sympathetically, as though she secretly thought it was amusing too.

"Look what I made," Amy said. She held up the frame showing an intricate collage she had designed using the dried flowers. "Do you like it?"

Saul nodded. "I do. It's very colorful."

Father stared across at Saul and Philip. "You boys had a good day?"

"Sure," Saul said. Then, before he could stop himself, added: "We missed you."

Mother looked up and smiled. "Isn't that nice, Frank. They missed us."

Father turned in his chair, frowning. "Sounds fruity. What you two been up to?"

Mother waved him away. "Ignore him, honey. We missed you, too."

Saul nodded, and listened to the gentle rhythms of the house; the burbling of the pipes, the rattling of the loose window upstairs, the welcoming hum of the family home.

As he stood there, a thought occurred to him, and he rushed upstairs and entered Philip's bedroom. It was much as he remembered it, but his heart was suddenly beating too fast: the clock was still in pieces on his brother's desk; the fabric of the mattress was still torn, exposing a tangled network of springs; and the drawing of the Fade was still hanging on the wall directly above Philip's bed.

He approached it with a sense of dream-like inevitability, already certain of what he would see, but forcing himself to look nonetheless. He peered at the picture and froze.

The lonely boy in the wilderness was gone. Instead, on a distant hill, seemingly set at an odd angle, was a single grey house; smoke was billowing from its chimney across the sky. In one of the windows of the second floor, pressed up against the glass, two faces stared out across the endless desert, one slightly smudged and unclear, the other as round as the moon. Their mouths were open in a soundless scream and their black eyes knew only pain and regret. The long days of waiting had begun.

Cemetery Dance Publications

Be sure to visit CemeteryDance.com for more information about all of our great horror and suspense eBooks, along with our collectible signed Limited Edition hardcovers and our award-winning magazine.

Our authors include Stephen King, Bentley Little, Dean Koontz, Ray Bradbury, Peter Straub, William Peter Blatty, Justin Cronin, Frank Darabont, Mick Garris, Joe R. Lansdale, Norman Partridge, Richard Laymon, Michael Slade, Graham Masterton, Douglas Clegg, Jack Ketchum, William F. Nolan, Nancy A. Collins, Al Sarrantonio, John Skipp, and many others.

www.CemeteryDance.com